Stolen Nights

RENEE HARLESS

Published by Harless Productions, LLC via Ingram Sparks

Cover design by Porcelain Paper Designs

Reader group: Renee Harless' Risque Readers
https://www.facebook.com/groups/reneeharlessrisquereaders/
Facebook: facebook.com/authorreneeharless
Amazon: www.amazon.com/Renee-Harless/e/B00VAHGAWE
Bookbub: www.bookbub.com/authors/renee-harless
Newsletter: www.reneeharless.com/newsletter
Instagram: @Renee_harless
Twitter: @Renee_harless
Snapchat: @renee_harless

Stolen Nights

RENEE HARLESS

Elle's life seems like one joke after the next.

Blindsided by a cheating husband? Check.
Ex-friend knocked up by said husband? Check.
Moving herself and two kids into a home willed to her by her estranged father? Check.
Disease infested fence separating her home from her neighbor's? Check.

That's the first thing to go. If only the gorgeous neighbor didn't rile her up every chance he gets and now with the fence gone she suddenly finds herself facing a new joke – that stupid heart of hers racing whenever he's close.

But one stolen kiss leads to a number of stolen nights leaving Elle with the choice of ending the fling before she gets hurt or checking another box off her "jokes on me" list – heartbreak.

Prologue

THE POUNDING INCREASES BEHIND my eyes as I watch my soon to be ex-husband smile wickedly across from me. We've been going through these proceedings for about six weeks, a constant back and forth that has increased my number of migraines exponentially. We make it one step forward and then two steps back.

My ex, Dan, is contesting everything. Nothing is making him happy.

Silently inside the maelstrom of my mind I keep asking, *"What does he want?"*

But, I know what he wants. What his endgame is. He wants everything of mine but without me. He wants an upgrade. An upgrade that comes in the form of my best friend.

She's five years younger than us at the ripe old age of twenty-five. I met her at the gym I frequented when she became a personal trainer. She and I built a great friendship and spent many evenings sitting at my home drinking wine and watching reality television. I had no idea that I wasn't the only one she was giving special attention to. Apparently riding my husband's cock was part of her personal training skills as well.

I just couldn't have a normal divorce. Nope. I had to have a whammy of a love tryst thrown in my path as well and it wasn't until I was handed the divorce papers that I learned my friend was a total of eight weeks pregnant with my husband's baby.

I rub my temples as another stack of papers is tossed in front of me which my lawyer angrily grasps.

We've been in this particular meeting for six hours already. Six fucking hours of my life gone. Poof! My ex is already getting the 3500-square foot house, which I put the down payment on, his vehicle, which I cosigned, and our dog. He didn't even put up a fight for our kids, which really set me off after our first meeting. He plans on having a new perfect family with Sky once she settles into my old home.

Right now he's fighting for the restored 1964 Mustang that was passed down to me by my grandfather.

He knows that it cost a pretty penny and he has the bargaining chip to get what he wants. Every time I shoot him down, he threatens to take the kids.

Dan is an investment banker with a steady job. He also has a gambling problem that I am certain Sky has yet to discover. He knows that he can pull his weight around, which is why we're using a mediator instead of a judge. My kids would be taken from me faster than Superman stopping a bullet if I used a judge.

Me? I'm just a baker that gets jobs based on online orders and word of mouth. It's not steady or a typical nine to five job, but I do well for myself, and I'm lucky that I have a trust left from my mother's parents to fall back on in an emergency. A trust that includes the car my ex is trying to get his grubby hands on.

Thankfully for me, I have one of the best divorce lawyers working on my team. She also happens to be my college roommate and about the only good thing working in my favor at the moment.

From her poised position at the head of the table Sara, my lawyer, boasts, "You can't ask for a vehicle that is part of my client's trust left by a family member. Nor can you continue to threaten my client by appealing to withdraw your signing over of the children. That paperwork has already been filed and approved by the judge. At this point, Mr. Sanderson, I suggest that you and your girlfriend take what has been graciously gifted to you and finalize this divorce. My client has given you practically everything you have requested and has asked for nothing in return but to get these proceedings over with. You continue to dawdle with the paperwork, and frankly, it's starting to irritate me. If you don't finalize these today, then I am going to have my client begin to request her own share of your property."

Dan shifts in his chair while his own lawyer tugs at the tie around his neck. He knows if I begin to fight, the house will be the first hurdle because it was essentially my office and I claimed the addition as such on our taxes. I'm still thankful that Sara had the expertise to take care of the child custody situation first when the proceedings began.

"Fine," Dan huffs as he leans over the table, Sky's poised hand resting on his forearm. The forearms I used to admire when he would help me roll out dough when we first got married. I loved the way they would flex as he pushed the rolling pin outward. Now as I stare at them, I want to throw up in my mouth a little.

Sara nudges my shoulder as she hands me a stack of papers to sign. As I finish each one, she places them in a manila folder then hands the pile to the mediator to make copies.

"These will be filed today, and you'll receive your copies in the mail in the next week or so. We will send your copies to your lawyer, Mrs. Sanderson," the mediator explains as he stands from the table. The look on his face shows how grateful he is that the meeting has adjourned.

I hang back in the room with Sara as Dan and Sky file out behind his lawyer without a backward glance. He got everything he wanted and more. The big house, the expensive car, the young pregnant wife – all of the things he once wanted with me.

The truth doesn't hurt as much as the intensifying burn knowing that at the age of thirty, I'm now divorced with two young children to take care of.

Turning toward Sara, I wince at the forceful gaze in her eyes instead of sympathy.

Her attitude toward me is like a Queen addressing her subjects. Strong, powerful, confident. "We need to discuss two other issues at hand now that the divorce is finalized."

A headache that was already forming turns itself into full blast at her words. We had been in talks about my biological father's home for the last couple of weeks, since his death. I didn't know him well, but he left me his home in his will, and it was his only possession. It is the perfect solution for me since I now have nowhere to live and the kids and I are tired of staying in an extended-stay hotel. We want a home.

"Okay. What's up?"

"Do you want the good news or bad news first?"

"Bad?" I ask hesitantly, because really, how much worse can my day get?

"So, while I've been working with a real estate lawyer to get the house switched to your name, we've come across an issue with the property."

The fear surges up inside me and I have to force myself to push it down. I blink at Sara in bewilderment and then ask, "What kind of issue?"

"There is a lien on the house due to a home equity loan used to pay off debt. It had been taken out with a bank outside of our area, that's why it wasn't listed on the paperwork. Being that the house was willed to you, it looks like you now have the burden of the lien unless you want the bank to take it over. And unfortunately, I think they may fight you on it. It's a good piece of property in a growing neighborhood, and I think you may be able to work with the amount."

"How much?"

She squirms in her seat as she flips through some paperwork. "It's, uh, significant. Almost as much as the house is worth."

"What am I going to do, Sara? I just gave Dan almost everything I have," I groan as stars dance behind my eyes. My clothes suddenly feel too tight, too constrictive. I need air.

She reaches out and grasps my hand on the table; her friendly hold is my lifeline.

"You're going to use some of the trust that you have left to pay it off. That will still leave you some money in the bank for a rainy day. You're going to try to sell the car if you want to put even more in your pocket, but I don't think that's necessary. And you're going to continue baking to your heart's content because you're amazing at what you do and your business is starting to take off."

Her words fuel me, and I feel the strength in each sentence. She's right. I'm not through. I'm not six feet in the ground yet. I've made it this far and I can do the rest on my own.

I smile over at her in thanks for the confidence she has in me and then she asks if I want to hear the good news.

"I'll take anything right about now."

"Well, I just need your signature here," she says, shuffling a piece a paper over to me. "Then I can file this for you with the social security administration. You will then have the pleasure of returning your last name to Knight."

"That's the best news I've had in weeks."

Chapter One

Elle

THE BRAKES ON THE faded white truck ahead of me begin to flash.

"This is it," I sigh, following the U-Haul trailer to the small brick ranch in the cookie-cutter neighborhood. Every house looks exactly the same as the next; the only distinguishable feature seems to be the paint on the door and shutters. So far the only thing that gives me a sense of peace is the older neighbors smiling and waving in my direction. Whatever issues my father had didn't seem to be with the neighborhood.

I haven't seen what my new place looks like. Sara never had the chance to show me pictures of the house or property and all I could find were browser searches on the internet. But even those weren't that good. I know it's shaped exactly like the others; the layout a mirror image of the homes on either side, and it has a decent sized backyard. Half an acre if my memory serves me right. Just big enough for the kids to play and for me to tend. Landscaping has never been my forte. Dan always paid for someone to come out and take care of the lawn for us, but the lawn now belongs to my ex-husband and my pregnant ex-best friend.

Finally the trailer in front of me brakes, and I pull into the single driveway that separates my property from my new neighbor behind a black Audi coupe. As I sit in my BMW SUV, one of the few consolations I requested in the divorce since I paid for it myself, I let the engine idle as I take everything in.

The house next door has a lawn greener than any I've ever seen before and a beautiful array of flowers in multiple colors lining the side of the driveway and the walkway on both sides. The shutters are a crisp blue, only a shade darker than the noon sky above. From the corner of my eye, I notice a cute copper birdhouse on a stand on the opposite end of the yard. Unfortunately, a nasty fence guards my view of seeing into the backyard.

With a deep breath I turn my attention to the house on my left, *my* humble abode. I shudder at the monstrosity before me. Overgrown grass and weeds dance across what would be a front yard and mask the walkway to the front door. The black shutters hang cockeyed from their hinges, grasping as tightly as they can, and some of the louvers are broken within the panels. One end of the gutters projects away from the roof making the home look condemned.

God, I hope it's not condemned.

A laugh trickles up from my chest, and I shake my head as I stifle a giggle. Of course this is the home my father would have left me. A familial kin I had only met twice in my life since he and my mother never married and parted on unhappy terms. I still wasn't quite sure why he left me this house to begin with, which seems to mimic my life at the moment. Rough. Jagged. Unkempt. I can only hope that what's inside reflects something warmer than the coldness I'm currently feeling.

I ponder my new life as I watch Sara in my side mirror as she jumps out from the U-Haul in a graceful dismount.

Maybe I can make the most of this. Maybe it won't be that bad. I have my health and my kids. That's what matters.

But my reality comes flying at me in the form of a pink sippy cup full of juice that slams into the side of my head, courtesy of my three-year-old.

Yep, that's the wakeup call I needed. My life is certainly no better than this dilapidated house outside my window.

I turn around in my seat and hand the sippy cup back to Kennedy. "Here, sweetie. Let's not throw things at Mommy."

"Sorry, Mommy," she says in return in a cute little voice that I can't ever stay mad at.

"Whelp, we're here, guys."

As he unstraps himself from his booster seat, my son Noah asks, "Where are we?" and pulls himself across the front seat to look out the big window.

"Remember how I told you and Kennedy that we were going to have a new home?" He nods as his face grimaces at the home.

"Well, this is it. This is our new home."

"I like the other home better. This one is ugly."

My heart breaks knowing that I'm taking the kids away from everything they've ever known. The pool that used to be in the backyard. The giant playground where they played with all the neighborhood kids. Right now all that I can offer them is a roof over their heads and some sweet treats.

"I'm sorry, sweetie," I say, running my hand through his soft brown hair and remembering the time when he got a hold of the scissors and took a chunk out. "But just think of the amazing things we can do to it. It's our own blank canvas, just like the ones you fingerpaint on. We can make it look however we want."

His eyes light up as he turns to look at me in excitement.

"We can do whatever we want?"

"Sure, within reason, of course."

"What if I want a dragon on my wall? Can I have a dragon?"

Drawing was never my strong point in school, but if Noah wants a dragon and that will make him feel at home, then by God I will give the kid a dragon.

"Absolutely. You can have a whole wall of dragons if that is what you want."

"Yes!" he shouts as he fist pumps the air, his tiny body filling the small space between the two front seats.

"And a playground and a pool?" he asks through a wide grin as his excitement rushes through his body.

"Well, we'll have to see about that. I'm not sure what the backyard looks like."

Summer is in full swing, so I had better look at getting something for the kids to occupy themselves with until I can get Noah into kindergarten.

I jolt in my seat as a knock sounds on my window, and Noah cackles loudly at my expression. I turn to look at Sara who shakes her head with a downturned face.

Stepping out of the car I say, "Hey," and then walk around the front to let Kennedy out of her seat.

"I didn't know it looked like this. The bank is the one that sent me the pictures. I would have had it cleaned up before I told you all to move in."

I take in the home one more time and then close my eyes. A deep breath fills my lungs, the scent of magnolia trees, flowers, and freshly cut grass swirling through my nostrils, and for a moment I feel resolute. I think that I can make this work. I can make this better. I can see its potential.

Opening my eyes, I look over at Sara dressed in a pair of pressed khaki shorts and a plain T-shirt as she nibbles on her lower lip. Even in worry, she is one of the most naturally beautiful women I've ever seen with her light blonde hair and porcelain skin.

"Sara, stop worrying. It will be okay. All I need is a lawnmower and a ladder."

"I'm sorry. I just wanted this to be better for you."

"I have a roof over my head in a good neighborhood. It could have been worse. Now, hand me the keys and let's go check out the inside."

At first, I am afraid I have spoken too soon and that the inside is going to be a nightmare, but as I turn the key in the lock and twist the knob, I'm surprised at the space before me – in a good way.

A gasp escapes my lips as I let Kennedy slide from my arms and down my body to the solid hardwood floors. "Wow."

"Well, at least you won't have to worry about anything in here," Sara adds, but my gaze is solely trained on the oversized kitchen across the way with an imposing island separating it from the living space.

It's almost too much for me to handle and I can feel the water pooling in my eyes. I may not have known my father, but I'm going to guess that I got my baking skills from him. The kitchen is a foodie's dream with its granite counters and butcher block island. White cabinets flank one entire wall of the space while the far wall has navy blue lower cabinets and white shelves on either side of a large window looking out to the backyard.

"Sara, these look like brand new cabinets and fixtures," I explain, still frozen in place at the entrance to the house.

"The bank said he had done some remodeling before his passing. I wonder if that was what the loan was used for."

"Hmm. . ." I murmur as I step farther into the room, glancing up at the pitched ceiling with dark stained wood beams cutting across.

"I don't understand why the inside is absolutely gorgeous, but the outside looks like it was forgotten."

Walking into the kitchen, I run my hand across the cabinets and then the stainless steel appliances that are identical to the top of the line versions I had at my old home. These cost a pretty penny.

Sara follows me into the kitchen area and parks herself onto one of the barstools at the island and rests her chin on her hands.

"From what I gathered, he knew his life was coming to an end – cancer. But he thought he had more time. He put you in his will when you were an infant so it was always his plan to give this home to you. And my guess is that he knew enough about you to know that you would want the space a certain way."

"I'm just so confused," I begin, turning toward her with an overwhelming feeling of loss surging through me. "This is a man I hadn't seen since I was a little girl. A man who left me all of this when I needed it most and had it set up the exact same way I would have done it myself. This isn't the man my parents ever spoke of."

"Well, maybe you should talk to them about it. Maybe they can shed some light on why they were estranged."

"I suppose," I agree as I nibble on my lower lip, visualizing where I plan to put all of my things. "I guess we should start moving things in. It's too bad your brother couldn't help us today."

"You don't want my brother's help, Elle. You know he'd just stare at you the entire time while pretending to lift the heavy stuff," Sara grunts as she talks about her over-muscled slacker of a younger brother that hits on me any chance he gets.

"Yeah, but maybe he would actually help if I batted my eyelashes and wore some short shorts."

"Don't be silly, Elle. He'd just follow you around like a lovesick puppy."

"True, true. Okay, well let me get the kids a snack and then we can get started," I say as I wander down the hallway in search of Noah and Kennedy. I find both of them in separate rooms connected by a Jack and Jill bathroom, sprawled out making fake snow angels on the fresh cream colored carpet.

"Hey, kiddos. Want a snack?" I ask, and they both jump up from their angelic positions and rush toward the kitchen.

Noah takes the vacant stool while Sara hoists Kennedy onto the other.

"I'll be right back. You both sit tight and be good for Miss Sara, okay?"

"Yes, ma'am," they reply, and I'm thankful every day that I have taught them good manners.

Back outside I walk toward my car and open the hatch of the cargo space to grab the small bag of groceries I picked up this morning. It's filled mostly with things for the kids and a few items for me to bake with. Tomorrow we'll have to hit the grocery store in full force, but tonight we'll order pizza– the kids' favorite.

As I struggle to close the door and keep the paper grocery bag in my arms, I notice the front door to my neighbor's house is open. A woman steps out wearing a short black cocktail dress, her shoes held precariously in her fingers, as her other hand reaches up toward a man standing in the shadows of his house. An arm full of tattoos stretches out to weave into the nest of the woman's dark red hair and it tugs her head back into the shadows.

An unfamiliar feeling pebbles across my skin as I watch the couple kiss and I wonder if my hunger for Dan ever resembled something like that. The need for that one last kiss before leaving for the day. The yearning to feel his lips against mine. I can't recall ever needing him like my last breath, and that thought sickens me.

Of course, during my gawking at the couple the bag I'm holding slowly slips out of my grasp until it crashes onto the pavement at my feet.

"Shit," I mutter as I bend down to gather the items and toss them back into the bag.

I look up just as the woman saunters across the yard toward her vehicle parked on the other side of the street, laughing in my direction. Anger boils inside of me, not at her laugh, but at her unwillingness to offer her assistance. A huff bursts from my mouth as I reach up and tighten the ponytail on top of my head and then grasp the bag in my arms as I stand.

My stomps are carried away in the breeze as I walk around the car, but as I reach the hood of my BMW,

I sneak a peek over at my neighbor's house. I can feel his gaze on me, even through the shadows, but I can't see his face. All I can see of my neighbor is the well-toned tattooed arm that has me wishing that I could see the rest of him. If only to see if he's tattooed in other places.

My mental images of him don't last long as his door slamming echoes across the yard and jolts me from my stance in the driveway. Continuing my journey, I walk back into the house and serve the kids each a bowl of applesauce and some animal crackers that they love.

"Alright, you two be good while Miss Sara and I unpack the truck, okay? When you're done with your snacks just leave them there until I can get a trash bag. Your tablets are in my purse, and you can play with them until I'm finished," I tell them, thankful I was able to have the electricity and internet restored before we moved in.

Sara and I work for a few hours and get the first round of items unloaded from the moving truck into the house before night begins to fall. I order the pizza, and the four of us sit cross-legged in the middle of the kitchen with our paper plates and cups of water.

The only rooms Sara and I made sure we set up were the kids' bedrooms and the bathrooms. I'll worry about my room another time. As long as they have their beds, then I'll make do.

"Alright, guys. It's late. So when we're done with dinner, I need both of you to get ready for a bath, okay?"

The kids nod with their puffed out cheeks full of dough, red sauce, and cheese at my request.

"You probably need to head out too. Don't you have to work tomorrow?" I ask Sara, realizing that it's Sunday.

"I do. I'm sorry we didn't get more done today. I can come back after work," she insists, but I shake my head. It's about time I start doing things for myself.

"I'll take care of it. I'm in no rush. And if I need help, I'm sure I could ask one of my neighbors."

Sara looks at me skeptically, one of her perfectly tweezed brows angling upward on her head. "I'm pretty sure they'd throw out their back. I know if I keep asking you I'm not going to get anywhere. I'll come back after work whether you like it or not. I already called an Uber and they'll be here in a minute." She holds up her phone with the Uber app pulled up.

"Fine," I say as we stand and I give her a massive hug, my arms squeezing her tighter than she probably expects as she lets out a puff of air at my attack. I'm not sure where I would be right now if it wasn't for Sara and her friendship. "Thank you for everything, Sara."

"Don't mention it. You'd do the same for me. Try to get some sleep tonight."

Escorting her to the door, I nod at her request and watch as she slides into the backseat of her Uber pickup.

Turning around, I gaze at my two kids looking up at me with excitement, worry, and love. So much love. And that's more than any amount of money I could have ever given my ex. The same ex that has signed over his rights to his kids and even asked that I change their last names.

Asshole.

They help me pick up the trash, and then I corral them toward the bathroom where I get all their nightly playthings and special bubbles ready in the hopes of making this transition as easy for them as possible.

Thankful that Noah and Kennedy are still young enough to bathe together, I wash them both down and then fill the bathtub with a few inches of water and about a foot of bubbles, just the way they like it.

Noah and Kennedy play in the bathtub with their bath crayons and ships while I sit on the lid of the toilet watching their little minds create a playful world. Just as I am about to pour a bit more warm water into the tub, the doorbell rings.

"Damn," I say under my breath so that the kids can't hear me. The doorbell rings again as if the user is pressing the button over and over.

"I'll be right there," I shout without a clue if the person on the other side can hear me or not. "Okay, guys. I need you to play nicely while Mommy goes to the door.

No heads under water and no pushing. Do you understand?"

"Yes, Mommy," they both reply as they look up at me with bubbles and water dripping down their faces, their big brown eyes locked on me.

"Good. I'll be right back," I explain as the doorbell continues to ring.

As I step out of the bathroom, I tread heavily to the door with a silent conversation rolling through my mind. I grip the knob in my hand and swing the door wide with every intention of giving the person a piece of my mind, but I swallow my tongue when I open the door to the owner of the heavily tattooed arm next door.

Without a greeting, the man with the tightly fitted black shirt snarls down at me. He must be at least six-foot-two because his frame towers over me and I have to tilt my head almost all the way back since I stand at about five-foot-three on a good day.

I'm lost in a spell; his blue eyes piercing through the darkness swirling inside me. It's hypnotizing.

"Move your car," he growls, and I have to shake my head to knock myself free from his trance.

"What?" I whisper, needing him to repeat himself.

"Move your car. You're blocking me in, and I need to leave."

"Excuse me?" I ask, perplexed as I angle my head in confusion.

"I'm sorry, but I don't know how else to explain this. Your car is blocking me in, and I need to leave."

"Oh," I say, feeling my eyes widen as he looks at me as if I've grown two heads.

Silence grows between us and I continue to stare at the gorgeous man in front of me, wishing he would turn uglier by the moment as he sneers.

Finally he breaks the stillness and asks, "So, are you?"

"Am I what?" I reply, only partly listening as I hear splashing in the bathroom, my mommy instincts on high alert.

"Are you going to move your car?"

"I can't do that," I respond as I turn in the direction of the bathroom just as four little legs carry two wet and soapy bodies across the hardwood floors. One arm is jutting in the air holding a Barbie doll out of reach.

I move away from the door and the gorgeous man just standing there as I chase the kids around the kitchen, praying that they don't slip and fall.

"But I need to leave. Move your freaking car!"

The two kids stop on a dime as they holler in unison, "Aw. . .," knowing that a bad word has been uttered in their presence.

I grip the set of keys in my hand as I snatch them from the counter and stomp toward the man standing at my door.

"You want the car to be moved so bad, do it yourself." I shove the keys into his well-muscled chest and I try not to gasp at the tingle I feel as my hand collides with his body. "As you can see, I am busy at the moment with something far more important."

He looks intently at me in confusion as he reaches up and takes the keys from my fingers.

"And watch your language around my kids," I tack on in spite as his gaze falls down to the keys with a heart-shaped charm dangling between his fingers.

He looks up at me just as I slam the door in his face and turn around to look at my soaked kids dripping water on the kitchen floor.

"Sorry, Mommy," Kennedy says as she shivers in the cold.

"Come on, guys. Let's get you dried off and into bed."

I walk them to the bathroom and snag two towels from the hooks and wrap each child in one, brushing my hands up and down the material in hopes of warming them up.

That night I tuck each child into their bed and read them their favorite bedtime story. Kennedy wants her favorite princess story and Noah wants *Star Wars*. As I turn off the light in Noah's room, allowing the small night-light in the corner to cast the room in a soft yellow glow, he looks over at me clutching his small bear in his arms.

"Mommy?"

"Yeah, sweetie?"

"Are you going to be happy here?" he asks, and my heart breaks as his concern is solely for me.

"Oh, sweetie. I will be happy wherever you and your sister are. You're all I need to be happy. I don't need a place for that."

He doesn't respond, but his small forehead crinkles as if he's trying to figure out some secret meaning to my words. Finally, he yawns and shimmies down farther under his sheets.

"I love you, Mommy."

"I love you too, Noah. So much."

Chapter Two

Jackson

IT'S BEEN A FEW days since I watched my new neighbor slam her door in my face. In her defense, I probably came off as a total asshole, but work called with an emergency and I had to get there as soon as possible. It's not every day that I get a call about a man trying to bench press weights that are way too heavy without a spotter. And of course, he happened to roll the bar to his neck, cutting off his windpipe.

She wasn't what I had expected when she opened the door. I had seen the long-legged blonde earlier in the day and had hoped that she would be a welcome distraction. Instead, I had come face to face with a haphazard brunette woman chasing her two naked kids.

I don't do baggage, and I don't do kids, and this woman looks like she has both of those in spades.

The house had been vacant for a few weeks since James, the previous owner, had passed away. He kept mostly to himself, and I only saw him if we were outside at the same time or if he needed a ride to the store. James didn't drive, so the driveway issue never came up.

I almost felt bad when she pulled up on Sunday to the overgrown yard and chaotic mess on the exterior, but after meeting the mousey woman the first time and feeling the wrath of her attitude, I felt less worried about the disorder.

I pull up to my house, having been away the last few days shuffling my time between my gym and my landscaping business, sleeping in whichever office I happened to occupy at the time. I notice that the U-Haul still sits on the street as an eyesore.

Her husband must be too lazy to unpack the truck for his family, I think to myself.

My Audi steers into the driveway behind her SUV, and I groan thinking about having to have a conversation with her about the parking situation, something I never had to do with James.

It's still early morning when I step out of my car, the bright pinks and oranges welcoming me as I gaze up at the clouded sky. The serenity of the moment washes over me as I take a deep breath and stretch my arms up to the sky, my shirt riding up exposing my low slung jeans. A gasp sounds to my right, and I look over to find my elderly neighbor still wearing her robe as she shuffles back toward her house in her slippers after grabbing the newspaper.

A smile rises across my lips thinking about how many times I have watched her scurry back to her home after seeing my chest exposed or a woman leave my house in the early morning. I'm not quite sure if she is set in her old ways or if she's remembering a time in her youth. Either way, it makes for some entertaining early mornings. Maybe tomorrow I'll try some naked yoga in the yard to see how fast she can scurry into the house or if she comes outside at all.

Shaking my head while I chuckle to myself, my early morning of relaxation is shot to hell when I hear a few grunts and then see a fence post go flying through the air. A fence post that separates our two yards.

I rush into my house, tossing my duffle bag in the entry, and make my way to the back deck where I see another piece of fence post leave the horizontal fence.

"What are you doing?" I shout, rushing over to her with clenched fists.

She peeks through the opening just enough so that I can see her dirt-smudged face and messed up hair pulled back into a knot on the top of her head.

"What does it look like I'm doing?" she retorts with a gloved hand on her hip. It rests on a pink T-shirt covering a pair of short denim shorts that showcase a pair of tanned and toned legs.

I'm a sucker for a good pair of legs.

I look up again and notice her mouth moving and her nose scrunched. I can't see her eyes behind her tinted safety glasses, but I'm going to assume she's pissed at me for something.

"What?" I ask, since I completely miss whatever it is she is yelling at me about.

And then she growls, probably meaning to sound ferocious, but it sounds more like a sweet kitten rubbing itself against my leg.

"I said, I am removing the rotten fence that just so happens to be on the flattest part of the yard."

The distraction of her stellar legs had pulled me away from my anger, but now it's returned with a vengeance.

"It's my fence!" I shout.

"And it's on my property. I had the line surveyed yesterday, and I want it gone. My kids want a playset."

She's right. I had an agreement with the previous owner because it was easiest to put the fence on the flattest ground. He didn't mind so long as I took him to the grocery store.

"You can't just tear out a fence that I spent money on."

"Yes I can," she argues, ripping another nail from the post in front of my eyes.

"Will you stop it?" I command as I hold the top of the post with my bare hands.

"No," she grunts in return, yanking at the post with all her might trying to free it from my grasp.

It's a dick move, I admit it, but I release my hold just as she pulls with all her might.

The move is classic as she falls backward, landing with a thump on her ass as she hits the ground. I'd almost feel bad about the fact that the board she had been gripping smacks her in the head, but as she screams out "Asshole!" loud enough to wake the rest of our neighbors, I can't help but grin as I watch her stand and wipe the dirt off her shorts.

She's a feisty little thing.

"You may want to reconsider tearing down my fence. I wouldn't want my assholishness to seep over to your side."

The woman rips her sunglasses from her face and tosses them to the ground as she comes to stand against her side of the fence. I imagine if the wood wasn't between us that she would be poking me in the chest with one of her glove covered fingers. She looks up at me, and I realize how pretty she really is. I hadn't noticed it too much the other night when I needed her to move her car. She has big brown doe-eyes surrounded by naturally long dark lashes. I bet she's never needed to wear mascara like most of the women I know. And her nose has a subtle upturn. But her lips. . .God, those lips are things men dream about. Not too small or too large. They pucker perfectly as she sneers up at me and then I remember, again, why I'm furious. This woman is making me lose my train of thought, and that does not sit well with me. The last time I couldn't keep my head on straight I almost lost everything.

"Look here. . ."

"Jackson," I add for her benefit.

"Jackson. My kids have been through hell the past two months, and all they've asked for is a playset. So whether you like it or not, my kids are getting a fucking playset today. I don't care if you strap yourself to the fence, I'll just remove you with it."

I almost feel sorry for her. . .almost. But as she gazes at me with disgust, not the lustful looks I'm used to, I narrow my eyes down toward her.

"Good luck trying, sweetheart. For every board you tear down, I'll just put one up."

"Is that a threat?"

"No, just a statement."

She opens her mouth to bite at me once more but then a crash sounds from inside her house, and I watch through the sliding glass door as two small kids, the ones I remember from the other day, work to pick up a chair that has fallen over.

Without a second glance, the woman drops her hammer on the ground and turns to walk away.

"Nice doing business with you, neighbor!" I call out as she reaches her deck.

She doesn't turn around, but she holds up a distinctive finger telling me what she really thinks about me.

"It's Elle, and this conversation isn't over."

Her name floats in my head, and I decide that I like it. It suits her.

"Oh," she calls out, the top of her body peaking out the door. "I need to go to the store, so move your car."

I don't get a chance to reply as she slams her door. I've won this round, so I go back to the driveway and park my car on the street.

See? I can play fair.

I sleep for a few hours as I try to catch up from the lack of shut-eye from having to work at my two businesses for the last few days. The landscaping hobby that has turned into a pretty lucrative business for me, my brother, and cousin the past few years is doing better than any of us had expected. I almost consider offering our services to Elle, but then I remember that it's been less than a week and she's already driving me crazy.

A loud grumble sounds in my bedroom, and I pat my flat stomach knowing that I haven't eaten since dinner last night. And most of that was burnt off in my office by one of the gym bunnies. Helga I think her name was. She was a trial member that came in with her friend Sylvie, whom I also know intimately.

From my naked state, I tug on a pair of clean gym shorts and make my way to the kitchen. I open one of the upper cabinets to grab a protein bar, and I do a double take as I look outside. A group of five overly muscled men stand in Elle's yard putting together a wooden playset, the fence long forgotten.

The protein bar dangles from my mouth as I step out onto my deck and scratch my head at the turn of events. One muscled man I probably could have set straight, but five? There is no way in hell I'd take that chance.

The sliding door opens, and it draws my attention as Elle walks out carrying a pitcher of lemonade. Her clothing from earlier is long forgotten, and instead, she wears a tight fitted black tank top and her cut off denim shorts. With her curves on display, I may actually need to go steal that pitcher of lemonade and drown myself in it.

She turns her head to glance over her shoulder, laughing at something the man behind her says. The square-jawed, heavily tattooed man has one hand pressed to Elle's lower back while another holds a stack of plastic cups.

An irrational surge of jealousy rushes through me, fueling my foolish anger toward my new neighbor.

As if she can sense me close by, her head turns in my direction and her smile morphs into a frown. It would almost hurt my feelings if I weren't infuriated by my lack of fencing and the man standing against her back.

"Where's my fence?" I shout across the yard, and all of the men halt their movements. Hammers and drills stop as all eyes turn to me.

Elle shoves her pitcher into the man's chest which he grabs reluctantly, his eyes piercing me and promising a world of hurt. Her steps are strong and steady as she approaches and for a moment I can feel my cock becoming aroused at the passionate look in her eyes.

She walks up the deck stairs and stops when she is no more than an inch from me. I can see a hint of sweat on her hairline, but as a light breeze drifts across our bodies, her scent fills my lungs, a mixture of vanilla, flowers, and sweat. The pulsing in my cock increases and I have to fight the erection forming in my shorts. I'm regretting I didn't tug on a pair of boxer briefs.

"Your fence? It's been picked up and tossed in the trash."

"What?"

"You heard me. And now my kids get something fun to help them transition a little easier," she adds, her pointer finger dabbing into my chest.

I stare at her a little perplexed and a whole lot turned on as smoke practically oozes from her ears. I don't know why this woman is so hell-bent on spoiling her kids. My mom always made it a point to teach my brother and I that you had to work hard for what you want. It seems like her and her husband are going to be raising the next spoiled generation.

From over Elle's shoulder, I watch the heavily tattooed man turn his head toward another female, the knockout blonde that I had noticed earlier in the week, as she takes the lemonade from his grasp. He drops his arms and turns toward the woman before making his way over to the playset to lift one of the two-by-fours up in the air.

Meaty showoff.

"No response?" she asks as she looks up at me with her big brown eyes, instantly bringing me back to the issue at hand.

"What?"

"I'm concerned. You started staring off into space, and I figured you'd have some sort of argument to continue."

She turns her head to glance over her shoulder, giving me an amazing glimpse of her sleek neck which I want to both strangle and suck on. Goddammit. As she turns back to me, her eyes light up with a mix of mischief and something else I can't really place. It vaguely resembles despair. But it's that twinkle in her eye that causes my alarm.

"I didn't peg you as one for the eye candy." She smirks as she steps to the side, opening my gaze to the handful of guys finishing up the playset.

"Eye candy?" I ask, confused until her meaning crashes over me. "You think that I like men?"

"I mean, why not? It's a good looking bunch. Can't say that I blame you."

My arm reaches out on its own accord and my hand latches onto her upper arm. I tug her and she twists back to face me, amusement splashed across her features.

"Elle, I'm not into men. I very much am a fan of the female body," I begin, and I feel a sense of triumph as her already heated skin from the sun blushes at my words. "Your muscled up husband was giving me the stink eye, that's all."

Her brows pinch closer together as her lips pucker. "I'm not married. Well, not any longer."

"Your boyfriend then."

"No boyfriend. Just my friend's brother and his friends."

For some reason, that revelation should make me feel better, but instead, it makes me more angered. What happened to leave this woman to fend for herself and her kids? Now that I know more of her story I really need to focus on distancing myself from her.

"Well, it seems that you have enough manpower to move that playset to another part of the yard and to rebuild my fence. I suggest you get started soon, otherwise you'll be working in the dark."

With new resolve, I spin on my heel and exit back through my sliding door, promptly locking it behind me. There is no telling if she is the type of person to follow me into my own home just to give me a piece of her mind. As I turn away from the glass, she pounds on it with the back of her fist shouting out a few names and choice words, but I continue back to my kitchen where I grab a bottle of beer and pop the top before making my way over to the couch.

My reprieve doesn't last long because one of our landscapers calls out of work sick and I need to find a replacement. A knock sounds on my front door. I slam my bottle so hard on my end table that I'm surprised the glass doesn't shatter.

With my hand gripping the doorknob, I wrench it open quickly while murmuring under my breath about missing a hockey game I had recorded.

"What do you want now?" I spew to who I thought was my neighbor, only to find my brother on the other side; my brother and his border collie.

"Well, isn't that quite a greeting?" He steps past me into my house, his dog Bailey following closely behind.

"I thought you were someone else," I say to my older brother, watching him swipe my newly opened beer and take a sip.

"Who did you think I was? Thanks for the beer, by the way." If it were anyone else, I would be snatching that beer right out of Cooper's grasp, but unlike many siblings, my brother and I get along extremely well, and I know that he works his ass off as a state police officer. We're only fifteen months apart, our parents wanting to have children close in age. A lot of people mistake us for twins because of our similar faces and builds, only our hair color differs.

"My new neighbor. In the span of five days, she's figured out how to drive me crazy and tear apart my yard."

He cocks his eyebrow, the same expression I have as Bailey hops up onto my couch and makes herself at home. Cooper notices and swats her gently on the behind to get her off. She makes a face as she lands on the rug and then walks around in a few circles to find her perfect spot.

"What do you mean?" He takes another sip of the drink and then walks over to the back door to peer outside. Without another word, he whistles in a low tone as he takes in the group gathered around the wooden playset bordering my yard.

I rest with my back against the countertop as he takes in the group, my attention locked on the refrigerator across from me.

"Your fence is gone," he states as if I hadn't just told him.

"No shit."

"At least you have a better view now," he mumbles under his breath. "Damn, you have all the luck."

What?

"All the luck?" I ask as I turn to look out the window where the men are grabbing all their tools, and the blonde is resting against one of the posts holding up a clubhouse attached to the playset. "No, not that one. That's just the friend. Satan's daughter is the brunette mess in the black shirt," I point out just as she comes around the corner of the clubhouse and begins climbing the wooden ladder. Her lean legs have Cooper and I, and the rest of the men outside, mesmerized as she climbs each rung. She gets to the top and jumps up and down with her arms raised high in victory, but I guess that she is secretly testing her weight to make sure that it's safe for her kids. And isn't that just the weirdest thought to have? I hate kids. I purposely don't offer a daycare at my gym to keep the rugrats out.

"Well, if Satan's daughter looks like that she can come destroy my life anytime."

I chuckle and then move back to the living room with a new beer that I snagged from the fridge along the way.

"I wouldn't wish that on my worst enemy."

"Dude, it can't be that bad. You haven't even been here the past few days."

"Exactly. She's already irritating me and I'm not even home!" I exclaim as I take a vigorous sip of my beer.

Cooper takes a seat on the couch and shakes his head with a half grin tilting the corner of his lips.

"What?" I ask, taking in his expression.

"Nothing. It just seems like you have the prime opportunity to scope out the resident hottie before anyone else."

"How'd you know she is single? I just found out about ten minutes ago."

Cooper shrugs his shoulders. "I looked for a glare on her finger. No wedding band."

Huh. Why didn't I think to do that?

I stew for a few minutes as Cooper takes hold of my television remote and turns on a sports channel.

"Oh," he adds. "I have night shift for the week. Do you think you can take Bailey for a few days?"

His mutt looks up at me at the mention of her name, and I swear she rolls her eyes and licks her lips. Bailey notoriously steals my clean boxers from my dresser. Even when I place them in the top drawer that sits about four feet high, she figures out a way to get inside.

But my brother works his ass off so I don't mind watching Bailey, though it may be slightly more difficult without a fully fenced in yard. But I wouldn't mind seeing Elle step in Bailey's dog poop if she happens to venture over that way.

"What has you smiling like the Grinch?" my brother asks.

"Oh, nothing," I lie. "I'd be happy to watch Bailey. But I'm going to need a favor from you before you leave tonight."

"What kind of favor?" he asks skeptically, and he has every right to be wary.

If Elle had the fence that separated our yard tossed out, then I'm going to make sure there is some sort of barrier keeping her from my space. It may also require a trip to a Home Goods store.

Chapter Three

Elle

UN BLANCHES THE SKIN on my face as it peers through the sheer curtains draped on the windows in the small bedroom. Guess I'll be purchasing some room darkening curtains soon. My old home had beautiful indoor shutters custom-made for all the windows. Shutters that my ex-friend is now enjoying. Knowing her, she has probably torn them down and hung up a hemp-based blanket in its place.

I hear the pitter-patter of footsteps as they scurry down the hall from their bedrooms and I shake my head to rid my thoughts of my previous life. Raising my arms above my head, I press my palms against my headboard and point my toes as I stretch out my body, my muscles sore from the work I put them through yesterday. Today is my last day to relax before I go back to working on my online baking orders.

A chuckle builds in my stomach as I recall the look on Jackson's face as he stepped outside and noticed the playset for my kids. It's as if he never actually expected me to continue to rip out the fence he placed on my property. Whelp, like so many other men before him, I was bound and determined to prove him wrong. Even if that meant enlisting the help of Sara's brother and his gym-rat friends.

I toss my covers aside, the white down comforter falling against the empty portion on my queen-size bed, and I grab my robe off the chair I placed in the corner. Peeking out from my door I listen closely, and as I hear a few giggles, I try to interpret their meaning. See, my kids have two types of laughs. One is the laugh which means they're genuinely enjoying something. The second and most dangerous laugh is the one that has a sneaky undertone because they're doing something they know they shouldn't be.

And, just like the rest of my life, it's that second laugh that reaches my ears, and I know that I'm in for a nightmare. I follow their giggles to the kitchen and hold back a screech when I find Kennedy standing on a stool reaching into the refrigerator and Noah pulling out all of my baking ingredients. Neither would be so bad if they both hadn't pulled out their Play-Doh cooking sets and strewn them across the floor.

With my arms crossed against my chest I move into the kitchen, making sure to strategically step over the wet balls of dough on the floor, and stand before my kids. They look up at me and blink once, and then twice, before slowly downcasting their gazes.

"What are you two doing?" I ask, trying to keep a level tone in my voice but probably failing.

"We were trying to make you breakfast," Kennedy insists as she moves down from the stool and over to where Noah stands.

"I appreciate that, but there is no need for this mess. What were you planning on making?" I bend down to scoop up the bags of flour and sugar before the water spilling from an overturned bowl seeps into the bags.

"Pancakes?" Noah asks as a question instantly giving away the kids' intentions.

Crouching in front of them, I look at their sad faces and remember that all of this is new to them as much as it is to me, and if they were simply trying to make me feel better, then I should give them the benefit of the doubt. Reaching my arms outward, I stretch them wide to accommodate their little bodies and tug them close. As shitty as my life has been the past few months, nothing can compare to the two children I have before me. In all of their sweetness and innocence, they inspire me to wake each morning with whatever bit of hope I can scrounge up.

"That was sweet of you guys to think of me. Next time, why don't we wait until I'm awake and I'll make pancakes, okay?"

"Okay, Mommy," Noah and Kennedy reply as I squeeze them a little tighter, letting their sweet baby scent fill my lungs.

Pulling back, I kiss the tops of each of their heads and ask them to clean up their mess while I whip up some of the pancakes they had promised, using my regular cooking supplies, not my baking supplies. Those are almost as precious to me as my kids, and they ensure our livelihood.

At the sink, I wash my hands and look out the window to the backyard and smile at the progress that I've made in about a week. I had the landscapers plant some flowers along the back of the fence, tulips to be exact. I've always loved how they open up in the sun, soaking in the warmth of the rays. Movement behind the kids' playset catches the corner of my eye, and I stare open-mouthed and dumbfounded.

He couldn't have stooped this low, could he? So much so as to hang a humongous brown tarp between our two properties?

"Kids," I shout. "Stay here. I'll be right back."

Noah and Kennedy both nod as they sit playing at their small table in the living room. I step out onto my deck wearing only my thin silk robe and matching chemise and shorts. Without a second thought I stomp over to the edge of the fencing post and unstrap the bungee cord holding the tarp and rope in place, then I do the same on the bottom and the other end. Now that I am closer to the driveway I look out and notice his car is missing. Good. As I fold the tarp, because, yeah, I'm still a thoughtful person, I consider calling the homeowner's association. I suppose if it continues to escalate then that will be the next recourse.

With the oversized tarp folded, I carry it over and place it on Jackson's deck. A dog barking inside startles me at first because I hadn't realized someone as mean and uncaring as Jackson had a dog. Much less could take care of it.

The dog comes to the back door and promptly sits as he looks at me, eyeing me up and down deciding if I'm worth the hassle or not. He and I stare at each other for a minute, and then the dog seems to smile before standing and moving back through the house. Weirdly enough it feels as if I've passed some sort of test.

Shaking my head, I walk back to my own house and finish up the pancakes I had started and get ready to begin baking. With my orders, I deliver on the same day or the next, so right now I only work locally and I have a few bakeries and restaurants that carry my items, but my goal is to take it nationally. I've had a few meetings with delivery companies and other bakeries interested in supplying the baked goods in my name.

Baking at this level was never my intention when I started. I worked as an administrative assistant and would bake when I would come home from work to release stress. The items that I would share with my coworkers were always a hit, and one of the vice presidents asked to take a pie home to his wife. Little did I know that she owned a chain of restaurants. With her help, my project took off from there.

"Guys, while you eat your pancakes I'm going to take a quick shower, okay? Noah, you can turn on the television when you're both done. I'll be right back."

"Okay, Mommy," they both respond and I watch as a large helping of syrup drips from Kennedy's mouth down onto the table. Guess I'll be removing a sticky mess later as well.

The bathroom in the hall is the one I have set up for me, my days of an attached master bath are long gone. It's still a step up from having to share one with the kids though. I remove my night clothes and place them on top of the hamper then step into the shower, turning on the warm spray. I know that I don't have long to indulge in a relaxing shower, so I hurriedly lather my hair and body then wash the suds clean. Luckily, I had a full wax a few weeks ago, so I don't have to spend time shaving, because I absolutely don't have time for that. I make quick work of conditioning my hair, this step is crucial if I don't want to spend an hour trying to brush it later. My hair has natural waves that tend to twist and frizz into each other every time it gets wet. Makes for a great time when I get caught in the rain.

I stand under the spray while the conditioner does its thing and close my eyes. The stress of the past few months sits heavy on my shoulders, and I really need to focus on getting more contracts for my baked goods, or I may have to look for a regular job. I'm lucky that my services pay well. Far more than I would have ever expected, but I'm afraid it may still not be enough. Sara had mentioned looking into catering, and I'm definitely interested, but I would have no idea who to contact to get my name out there.

Unfortunately, the shower does little to relieve my anxiety, and as I wash out the conditioner and step onto my bath mat, I realize that I had forgotten to bring in a clean towel from the linen closet.

"Shit," I curse. I wonder for a moment if Noah is big enough to grab me a towel and decide to try my luck. "Noah!" I shout, waiting for a reply, but none comes. "Noah!" I repeat and receive the same response. Concerned, I stick my head out of the door and look down the hall hoping to spy the kids watching television but the screen isn't on.

In a panic I grab my thin, pale pink robe and toss it over my body, tightening the tie a little more than necessary. I hurry to peek in the bedrooms hoping to find them in one of the rooms but I come up short.

In my dash to find my kids, I stub my toe on the leg of the end table as I move into the living room, but my pain is quickly forgotten when I find my front door wide open. My heart lurches in my chest, and if I didn't know better, I would think I am having a heart attack.

I barely notice that most of my body is exposed by my flimsy robe as I race out the front door screaming my kids' names.

"Noah! Kennedy!"

At first I don't see them, but then I hear the light giggles that only a mother would recognize. I run through the grass of my front yard and across the driveway, paying no mind to the fact that a second car is parked behind mine.

"Noah! Kennedy!" I scream again as I round the back edge of my car and come to a complete stop. In the front yard of Jackson's home, I find my two kids and the dog from earlier rolling around in the grass, both Noah and Kennedy donning their pajamas.

I bend forward, hand on my rapidly beating heart, as I take them in, their laughter filling a void in the empty space of the pounding muscle.

"You should probably remember to lock your front door if you leave your kids alone," a deep voice rattles from close by. It's then that I peer up and notice Jackson sitting on the steps of his front porch eyeing me disdainfully.

"Excuse me?" I gasp at his harsh tone.

He slowly rises from his perch and meanders his way toward me as if he hadn't just insulted me as a person and a mother.

"I simply suggested that you may want to make sure to lock the doors if you're going to be leaving your children alone for any portion of time."

"The doors were locked. I assure you," I argue as the fire begins to build inside of me.

"Obviously not if your kids are outside right now and you didn't know where they were," he adds as he stops in front of me and trails his eyes up my body, my skin prickling under his gaze. I watch in fascination as the tip of his tongue peeks out between his lips as his gaze lands on my breasts, but it doesn't linger. Jackson brings his eyes to meet mine and the heat swirling within them is electric.

I'm unsure if it's the moment catching up to me, or the way I can feel an attraction for him blossoming, but

I feel out of my element and I immediately go on the defensive.

"I can assure you, Mister. . . "

"Divers," he interjects.

"I assure you, Mister Divers, that my children were not left in an unlocked home."

Jackson doesn't respond, he merely cocks his dark eyebrow, highlighting his gorgeous blue eyes, of course, and crosses his arms against his chest.

"Noah?" I begin without taking my eyes away from Jackson's. "How did you get outside?"

"Um, I got the chair and twisted the lock thing. It's easier than at our other house. We saw the dog outside and wanted to play."

"Didn't I ask you to stay inside until I was done?"

"Yes, ma'am. Are we in trouble?" he asks, and I can hear the tiny quiver in his voice. Both of my kids hate being in trouble and they're usually very good, but I know my rules are hard to go against a dog playing outside. They've been asking for a puppy since our neighbor at our last home got a golden retriever.

"Yes, you are," I say as I smirk up at Jackson whose eyes haven't left my face. His penetrating gaze is doing something to my body that I haven't felt or recognized in years; not since I got pregnant with Kennedy. I feel desired. My nipples pebble on their own accord and I'm too afraid to move from this spot, too afraid that I'll launch myself at this infuriating man. Between the heat of the summer, and the heat of his stare, I feel myself surrounded by dizziness.

"I guess that answers that, Mister Divers," I say, but my voice sounds like a breathless whisper to my own ears. I can't imagine what it sounds like to him. I force out a cough, hoping to cleanse my throat and speak more clearly. "I didn't realize that you had a dog."

"I don't. Just dog sitting. I didn't realize you were so good at folding a tarp." His deep voice throbs across my skin leaving tiny goose bumps in its wake.

"Well, I like to think I'm multitalented," I jest saucily. "Next time it goes up I'm contacting the HOA. I don't think they'd take kindly to it."

"Step on my lawn again and I'll call the cops. Got that, sweetheart?" Jackson says as he leans toward me slightly. His masculine scent mixed with his cologne and a hint of perfume churns around me.

I'm about to speak up and give him a piece of my mind when his eyes dart toward the road and then back at me. Jackson leans closer to me, his mouth just beside my ear, his nose touching my wet hair. Then I feel it. The brush of his finger against my skin, just under the lapel of my robe.

"You may want to head inside unless you want to give my parents a show. I can see your nipples through your wet robe," he says, and at first I am stunned into silence, but then I glance down to where my pale pink robe has gone completely see-through. My wet hair is draped over my shoulder and the droplets of water have soaked the thin silk exposing the tip of my breast to him.

In a moment of embarrassment, I glare up at him in shock as he moves away from my face and stands straight. I'm not even in shock that my breast is exposed. After having two children that I nursed for the first years of their life, I have very little modesty left. My excitement comes from the spark that I felt at his touch. The way the rough tip of his finger caressed down my soft skin leaving a heated path along my chest.

I step away from Jackson, my mind whirling with the implications of how much I crave his touch. How much I want him to repeat that sensation all over my skin. Without a second glance, I turn around and grab each of my children's arms, dragging them back to our house a bit more harshly than I should, but in my embarrassment and receding panic, I am having a hard time controlling myself.

"What did I tell you both about leaving the house? What if a bad man took you away from me?" I whisper to Noah and Kennedy with a distinct quiver in my voice as we step onto my front porch.

They both look up at me with sadness and worry, and it hurts my overly pounding heart. As a mother I have feared for them every day since the moment I saw the two pink lines on the pregnancy tests. But now, guiding them through life as a single mother, I am terrified that I won't be enough for both of them, that I won't be able to protect them the way I need to.

The kids don't respond to my question, and as they step into the house, I faintly hear Jackson's voice from next door as he greets someone. His tone is warm and loving, something I haven't heard from him before. I chance a glance over at him and I'm surprised to see him hugging a woman with short blonde hair and a tweed jacket paired with dark denim jeans. I feel disgusted remembering the scent of perfume on him as we sparred not too long ago and the way he trailed his finger across my breast. But as he pulls away from the woman he looks up and winks in my direction, as if he knows I have been watching.

"Come on, Mom, I'll make you some breakfast," I hear him say, and my cheeks fill with warmth.

Shaking my head, I complete my journey back into the house and lock the door behind me. Guess I'll be going to the store today to get some special locks that the kids can't pick.

Kennedy and Noah both trail behind me with their "shopper in training" carts as we walk down the aisles of the local superstore. I need to look for some clothes for the kids for when they start kindergarten and preschool this fall and find those pesky locks I read about online. I'm used to buying their clothes at high-end retailers where I'm not having to sift through mountains of items to find a size, but I am grateful that I can afford any clothes for them at this point.

I sent Dan a message after the fiasco this morning with the kids leaving the house to see if he wanted to chip in for new clothes, but of course, I only received the one-worded answer – No. His lack of concern for the kids leaves me wondering if he'll even keep up his side of the court-ordered monthly visitation.

My phone buzzes in my back pocket as I hold up a unicorn shirt for Kennedy who nods enthusiastically and grabs it from my hand to toss in her cart. Pulling the phone out I notice a text from Sara.

Sara – What are you and the munchkins doing?
Me – Shopping. I never realized how expensive
**   kid's clothes are, even at the superstore.**
Sara – Sorry. Want to grab a drink to drown your
**   sorrows? I'll drive.**
Me – I can make you dinner.

**Sara – How about I treat you guys to dinner?
You deserve a break.
Me – You sure you can handle the madness?**

Typically, when Sara and I would go to dinner, there would be no Dan and no kids because we had a nanny that lived close by.

**Sara – I think I can handle it.
Me – O'Malley's at 5:30? The kids like the Irish
  nachos.
Sara – See ya then.**

As I close out the messenger app, I notice a missed call from my mother. I haven't spoken to my parents, my mother and my stepfather, since they fought me against the divorce. They insisted I stick by Dan and help him raise his new child, and when I told them that I'd rather stab myself with a needle under my toenails then help him raise his child with someone else, they balked. And top that off with the fact that they painted my father to be some madman, even though he had renovated his house to suit my needs before leaving it to me, left me confused. Not that they try to reach out often since they live about four hours away, but when she had called earlier I couldn't bring myself to answer. I'm not sure if I'll have the strength to answer again for a while. Though I need to send out invites to Kennedy's fourth birthday party next weekend and I'll need to invite both them and Dan and Sky. Good times.

This reminds me that I need to stop by the party aisle to grab some invitations. There is something to be said for everything being located in one store.

I help the kids grab a few more shirts and pants before I make my way toward the invitations where I snag the unicorn invite Kennedy is staring at in wonder.

"You sure you want unicorns, baby? This is your last chance."

"Yes, Mommy. I want the unicorns. I love them!" she projects loudly, drawing the eyes of a few people walking by, including our new neighbor. At this point, I am concerned that he may be stalking us, but then I remember that this is the closest store to our neighborhood.

He looks over at us as he passes by carrying a pack of bottled beer just as Kennedy begins to do her potty dance.

"I gotta go, Mommy," Kennedy cries as she tugs on the edge of my shorts.

"Can you wait until we get home?" I ask as I look at our full carts and then back over to her.

"No. I gotta go now!" she protests.

"Fine, okay."

I look up front wondering where I can leave the carts so I can go past the registers, then I hear his deep voice.

"There is a family bathroom in the back," he offers as he stands at the end of the aisle.

I glance up at him surprised that he is offering any assistance to my situation. He's made it very clear that he despises me as much as I despise him. But as Kennedy starts bouncing on her toes, I know that we don't have much time left.

"Thank you!" I exclaim as we rush past him, me tugging two carts while Noah and Kennedy try to keep up with my pace.

"You're welcome," he shouts as we pass, but I pay him little mind. I have a three-year-old with a dire need on my hands.

With one crisis averted, I turn my attention to the two scoundrels sitting across from me at O'Malley's. They hide their nefarious ways beneath layers of cuteness and sparkles.

I don't notice Sara's approach as I harness my gaze on my kids sitting across from me innocently coloring their sheets from the hostess, wondering where I have failed as a mother.

"Why do you look so gloom and doom?" Sara asks, sliding into the booth next to me.

"Look at them, all sweet and innocent."

I watch as her gaze narrows on Noah and Kennedy as she searches for something out of character but then shrugs her shoulders.

"Yep, as cute as always."

"Did you know that I am raising criminals? Those two faces are going to be on mug shots one day."

Her melodic giggle drifts past me and falls on deaf ears. I'm too mortified and humiliated to partake in her laughter.

"What did they do?" she asks after ordering a margarita from the waiter.

"You know that we went to the store to begin shopping for school clothes." She nods then I continue. "Well, while we were in the party aisle my sweet innocent children snuck one past me. It wasn't until I was leaving the checkout station that I noticed each of them was holding a stuffed unicorn." I look over at Sara, and I'm surprised to see a smile on her face instead of the frown I expected. She is a lawyer after all. "They stole them, Sara. My own children are thieves!" I say in horror as I rest my head on the top of the table just in time for the waiter to return with my beer and her margarita.

"Well, what did you do when you found out?" she asks as she opens up her menu.

"I marched them right up to customer service to pay for them. And you know what happened? They told me not to worry about it. Not to worry!" I emphasize. "My children stole and they told me not to worry about it. What kind of world are we living in that people are okay with children stealing unicorns?" I ask her, slamming my fist on the table, alarming the couple sitting at the table across from us, the older woman furrowing her brows in distaste toward me.

"I think you're being a little overdramatic. You did the right thing trying to pay for them. That's all you can do. And I'm sure you've spoken to your sweet angels about the repercussions of stealing."

"Yes, of course. I told them that if they steal again they'll end up in jail. And jail is far more boring than their grandmother's house on a rainy day."

"That would put the fear in any child."

I shrug as I rest my chin in the palm of my hand as my elbow props it up on the table.

"So, what's new with you?" I ask Sara. Even though we live closer to each other now, I still don't see her as frequently as I would like. She's one of the top lawyers in her office and she's up to make partner this year, so she has been working a lot more than normal.

"Nothing much. I have a meeting with the President this week. Hopefully, it will be good news. I'm tired of busting my butt and getting nothing in return."

"What happens if you don't get a promotion?"

"I. . . I don't know. I'll probably start looking for another firm to work for. I'm getting tired of feeling underappreciated."

"You deserve something better." I let the sentence hang in the air.

And so do I.

The kids perk up across from me and start waving madly in the newcomer's direction behind me. I turn my head to see what has garnered their attention and I wish that I hadn't. Jackson is stalking past us behind the hostess with another man that looks eerily like him, only blond.

"I swear I think he's stalking me," I mutter under my breath as I take a gulp of my beer, the coolness and hint of citrus a welcome relief.

"Who?" Sara pivots in her seat. "Oh, the new neighbor. Who is that with him?"

"Don't know. Don't care. This is the third time I've seen him today, and it is three times too many."

"Hmm. . ." Sara adds as the men walk past, Jackson taking the time to wave to my kids which would typically melt my heart, but it's still frozen solid after Dan.

"Hmm. . . what?"

"I just think you protest an awful lot regarding your very sexy neighbor."

"You think he's sexy?" I ask, my nose scrunching on my face as if I've smelled something terrible. And I have – my lie. Jackson is more than sexy. He's gorgeous with his tanned skin, tattoos, and dark hair that seems to be in permanent disarray. But I can't tell Sara that. Because even though he's gorgeous and he makes my pulse race, he's still a thorn in my side.

"Uh, unless you need your eyes checked, every female in this establishment thinks he's sexy. Just look," she points out.

My gaze travels around the room and I notice that every woman and a few men are checking out the duo as they're led to a table in the corner. Even the young hostess lingers a little longer than normal as she places their menus in front of them. And of course, Jackson takes the seat directly in my line of sight, probably just to piss me off even more. Damn him and that smirk as he notices my attention is on him.

"Ugh, I wish he would just leave me alone." Slamming my menu closed I slouch against the back of the booth, but I swear I can feel his chuckle against my skin, even from this distance.

"I wish you would take the opportunity as it presents itself."

"And what opportunity is that?"

"Sex. He looks like the kind of man that knows what he's doing in bed and you're right next door. Just ask him if he wants tacos one night then take him to your personal buffet."

"Oh my gosh, what is wrong with you?" I murmur in alarm as I glance at my kids happily coloring their sheets as I stifle my laugh.

"I probably need to get laid too," she adds just as the waiter steps up to the table to take our order. "Hey handsome, are you up for the task?" she asks our adolescent server who promptly blushes and cowers into his little notebook.

I give our order to the waiter who nods over and over again and then scurries away without a backward glance.

"I think you scarred him for life." I take a sip of beer and play a game of tic-tac-toe with Noah.

"I think that guy may be your rival's brother, I should ask him. He looks like he'd be good with his hands."

"What makes you say that?" I pause and look up from my game to see Jackson's attention on a svelte blonde leaning against his table.

"Because I think I've had them on me before," Sara whispers as she stares at the back of Jackson's guest's head in full concentration.

Chapter Four

Jackson

HE BAR COMES CLOSE to my chest before I push it upward above my body. My arms quiver as I complete my fifteenth rep of the chest press.

"Man, what has you so fired up today?" Cooper asks as he helps me lift the bar and weights back onto the rack.

The sweat pours down my face, back, and chest as I sit up on the bench. Cooper tosses me a towel and I wipe myself clean before reaching for my bottle of water. My gym is quiet this time of the morning. I try to get here around four or five in the morning on the weekends because the place fills up fast. And to be honest, since my new neighbor has moved in, I haven't been getting much sleep. I don't want to think that my dreams of her are the reason, but I'd just be fooling myself.

"Nothing," I reply.

"It's not nothing. You've been on edge since we got here this morning. And to be honest, you were on edge last night at dinner too. Especially when we saw your. ..new neighbor," he adds, as if a light bulb has gone off above his head.

"What are you saying?" I ask as I stand and wipe down the bench before my brother swaps the spot with me.

He reaches up and takes the bar in his hand before bringing it down and then pushing it up into the air. With a grunt, he says, "What I'm saying is. . . that it's interesting how you've become so worked up since your new neighbor moved in about a week ago."

"I think you're imagining things. If anything has me worked up, it's owning two businesses and not enough staff."

He looks up at me from the bench with a bullshit expression as he completes another set. "Well, then look at hiring some more people. I know both are doing well enough that you could hire a manager for each and you wouldn't have to do all the paperwork that you despise so much."

"Yeah, I should probably start hiring some people."

"And I still think it's your neighbor," he growls as he pushes the bar back on the rack.

"Believe what you want," I add, smacking his shoulder and head back to my office to go through the payroll from last week.

Half an hour later my head hurts from having to fix a few employees' hours and wondering why my staff at the lawn service aren't clocking in at all. I take pride in hiring people that have the best resumes, but I believe I may need to go in another direction. It seems this week I'll be laying off an additional three people – two from the gym and one from the lawn service.

Looking up from my computer, I'm surprised by the woman standing at the front desk across from my office. Elle is wearing a tight pair of gray athletic pants, no different than some of the others that come into my gym, but on her, they show off her toned thighs and behind. Just gazing at the curve of her ass has me wanting to take a bite of her juicy bottom.

She wears nothing else but a sports bra that has different straps crossing this way and that way, almost as if they are creating a barrier around her body, cocooning her skin from onlookers. But Elle is mistaken if she thinks she won't draw attention to herself. Even outside of her attire, her long hair is pulled up onto the top of her head in a ponytail, the ends curled and resting between her shoulders, showcasing the beautiful lines of her slender neck.

Elle must feel my stare on her because her head abruptly turns in my direction and she pins me with her surprised gaze. I tilt my head down and close my eyes as I try to calm myself before her approach, because even without seeing her, I can feel each step she takes, bringing her closer to me.

The door to my office hesitantly opens and then is quickly followed by a soft closing, as if she's being precautious about her entrance. She's right to think I may throw her out. We haven't had the best rapport thus far.

"Hello, Jackson. I can't say that I'm surprised to see you here."

I look at her directly and let my eyes roam over her body and watch in fascination as she tries to mask a shiver, not from the chill in the air but from the sensation of my gaze on her skin.

Leaning back in my chair I cross my arms against my chest. "Well, you are in my gym, so forgive me if I am surprised to see *you* here."

Wonder flashes in her eyes and I'm secretly pleased that I have been able to make that look cross her face. I'll mark that as an achievement for the day.

"Oh. This is your gym?" she asks and I nod, watching as she sucks her lower lip into her mouth, biting the soft flesh with her teeth.

"The question is. . .why are you in my gym on an early Sunday morning?"

"My friend Sara offered to take my kids to church with her and her family so I could get back into my routine."

"That was nice of her, but you didn't answer my question. Why my gym?"

I try not to laugh as she stomps her foot lightly and huffs in place.

"Obviously I didn't know it was your place. Otherwise I wouldn't have come here, and frankly I'm regretting my decision as we speak."

"Chill out, sweetheart. Unless you want to go to the gym thirty minutes away, we're the closest one to your house."

"Do you get off on giving me a hard time?"

I shrug my shoulders as I reply, "A little. Did Jeremy get you all set up?"

"No, not yet."

"Have a seat and I'll get it taken care of."

Ten minutes later and learning far more about Elle and her physicality than is probably necessary by her neighbor, we finish up her gym paperwork and she signs a year contract. My gym isn't the cheapest or the most advanced, but I pride myself on our personal trainers and knowledge.

"I heard through the grapevine that you offer a sunrise yoga class and that it's very refreshing. Who's the teacher and where can I sign up?"

"Well, it's offered every day, and the trainers take turns opening the class. It's actually everyone's favorite. A lot of our members do it after some strength training, so we run it around seven in the morning. And as far as the teacher for today, you're looking at him."

"You do yoga?" She takes in my body from head to toe as I stand from my chair and move around my desk.

"There are a lot of things about me you don't know, sweetheart. Now, if you don't want to be late to the class we better head over to the studio."

I start the class as normal for a Sunday because it's been my routine for as long as the gym has been open, which is roughly five years. I have a bachelor's degree in business management but I am also a certified personal trainer, something that helped pay the tuition while in college. The lawn care business came up just as a need arose in our area and my brother and our cousin Hunter do our best to manage it and our three employees.

I lead the class into a few cat and cow positions and then we move into a few sunrise salutations followed by the warrior poses. After the first round, I walk around the room adjusting a few of the member's poses so that they are feeling the full effect of the stretch. As I make my way over to Elle, I'm pleasantly surprised to see her transition from a perfect downward facing dog into a warrior one stance. Her body moves in one synchronized motion, no wobbling or readjusting needed. Which is unfortunate for me because I want to get my hands on her more than I've wanted anything for a long time.

The class glides into another salutation and I move toward Elle without a second thought. Her body shifts into another downward facing dog and before I know it I'm standing behind her, my legs on either side of her body, and my hands firmly digging into her hips as I adjust her stance unnecessarily. At my touch, her body goes slightly limp and I hear a soft sigh escape from her lips.

Of course, my momentary lapse in judgment doesn't go unnoticed because none other than Chelsea, one of the gym bunnies, asks me to adjust her stance as well. I squeeze Elle's hips as she moves back into warrior one and then help Chelsea as she pretends to struggle with the transition. I know she's pretending because she attends this class without fail every Sunday.

I head back to the front of the class and take them through a few more stretches before I conclude the session. A few of the attendees speak to me about the class and really just to catch up for the week. A few are husbands and wives or ex-military, which are my favorite kind of attendees. As I speak with one of my older veterans I consider reaching out to a local military group that specializes in finding jobs for their veterans. I make a mental note to contact them tomorrow.

Out of the corner of my eye, I watch as Elle performs a few more stretches and then begins rolling up one of our extra mats. As I am about to go over to her I feel a hand on my arm and I look over my shoulder to see Chelsea sidled up beside me.

"Hey, Jackson," she purrs, and I look at her just as she licks her plump lips.

"Hey, Chelsea," I reply, removing her hand from my arm and taking a step back. "Did you enjoy the class?"

Boldly she steps toward me, brushing her breasts against my arm. "I like everything that you do. How about you come back with me to my place and we can practice a few more moves in my bed?"

I ignore her question and instead watch in fascination as Elle rolls her eyes and steps out of the room.

Trying to be a gentleman, I turn toward Chelsea and let her down easily. Normally I would join her back at her place for an afternoon workout, but ever since Elle moved in I can't imagine warming anyone else's bed. Which is a damn travesty for me and my bachelorhood.

I watch as Chelsea retreats from the room with her head held high and approaches one of the other personal trainers, most likely to give the same offer. There is a reason she's considered a gym bunny.

Stepping out of the room, I search for Elle and find her in front of the mirrors with a set of dumbbells performing hammer curls. I walk over to her and she never loses her focus on the mirror, but I know she has recognized my approach because her movements become quicker, more staggered.

"Hey, you know if you slow down the movement as you go down you'll get better results."

"Thanks," she huffs as she continues her reps.

I continue to watch her, staring at her slender arms as the muscles bunch with each curl.

Finally, she sets the dumbbells back in the rack and turns toward me with her arms across her chest.

"Did you need something?"

"I was just wondering if you enjoyed the class."

"I did. Thanks. Now isn't there another woman you can go bug?"

"Why? I'd much rather bug you," I insist, causing her to roll her eyes, those beautiful brown irises shifting behind her lids.

"That's too bad, I'm leaving. Thanks for signing me up. Hopefully we won't run into each other again," she boasts as she grabs a spare towel and wipes her face before tossing it in the bin.

I spend the day at the office paying bills and writing up the schedule for the gym for the week. I also take a few minutes to speak with my parents. Ever since Mom drove up on a half-naked Elle in her soaked bathrobe, she's been peppering me with questions about my new neighbor.

Shutting down my computer, I think back to how she looked as she rushed over to my yard, having spotted her kids. At first, I hadn't noticed her lack of dress. From my perch on the porch I was stunned by the look on her face, the utter horror at the thought that her children had been taken. I watched in fascination as her features softened at seeing them play with Bailey.

Unfortunately, I wasn't able to control my assholishness. Maybe it was my attraction to her that fueled me, or simply the fact that I had spent the better part of the night at a bar with my cousin Hunter fending off women, but I was irritable and wanted her attention on me. There was only one way I knew how – enter asshole.

We'd been in close proximity before, namely that night I needed her to move her car and she shoved the keys into my chest, but yesterday as I leaned into her I couldn't help but reach forward and touch her damp skin. I had tilted forward to whisper in her ear and I inhaled her shampoo – a mix of vanilla and strawberries. I was drunk on the scent, and in my intoxication, I had reached out and stroked her soft skin beneath her robe, my vision clouded by her pale pink nipple poking through the damp silk.

Just remembering that interaction yesterday has my cock swelling beneath my jeans. Luckily I'm saved from further embarrassment as the young guy manning the front desk asks if we're ready to close up. Typically the gym only stays open until nine at night, but we stayed a little later to accommodate a few members finishing their circuits.

"Ready to close up, boss?"

I look up to my office door and nod, then I stand from my desk and turn off the light in my office. My gym and the night sky may be dark as I head to my car but my mind is washed in light. A light I only seem to have when I think of my pesky neighbor Elle.

The drive home is long and boring. The volume on the radio is turned up louder than one should probably need, but when I turned the knob I was hopeful that I could drown out my thoughts – it has not been successful.

Finally, my house comes into view and a smile grows on my lips. I've been working nonstop for the past two weeks and tomorrow I have a very rare day free. But as I get closer to my driveway, I notice a small white coupe parked behind Elle's SUV.

Dammit, I mentally groan. I thought I gave that woman a clean brush off at the gym, but it seems Chelsea is looking for a repeat from me come hell or high water.

I pull my car onto the side of the road with the hope that I can get Chelsea to leave quickly but as I approach my front porch, I know that won't be the case. She sits slumped in one of the chairs on the front porch with a bottle of vodka in her hand. A half-empty bottle of vodka.

Using my hand, I nudge her shoulder as I remove the bottle from her grasp and she promptly slumps to the other side of the chair. Anger begins to boil inside of me. I've had a long enough day and all I wanted to do was come home, heat up some dinner, and watch a game. Now I get to babysit.

"Chelsea," I growl as I perch against my porch post waiting for her to come back from unconsciousness. She begins to move slightly, so I nudge her foot, which earns me an indistinguishable noise from her direction.

"Hmm. . .?" she asks as she begins to sit up in her seat and open her eyes.

"What are you doing at my house, Chelsea?"

"Why are you yelling?" she asks as she presses her hands to the side of her head.

"I'm not yelling. I'm simply asking you why you thought it was a good idea to come to my house while I was gone and drink on my porch."

I pin my gaze on her hoping to use some of the skills my brother possesses in getting answers from people. Chelsea squirms in the seat before bringing one of her fingers to her mouth and chewing on the tip.

"Chelsea?" I reiterate hoping to rid myself of her presence sooner rather than later.

She pushes herself from the chair quickly, standing almost to my height with her sky-high heels. I notice she's barely dressed in a short dress that looks more like a man's tank top.

"Jackson, I thought we had such a good time last time we were together. Don't you agree?" she purrs as she gently strokes one of her fingers down my bare arm giving me chills. And not the kind of chills that are welcome. The kind that makes me wonder why I slept with her in the first place. Chelsea is gorgeous, but I usually don't rely on looks alone. I may have been off my rocker that day.

"Believe what you want, Chelsea, but there will be no repeat. Let me call someone to pick you up. I don't want you driving."

"Jackson," she whines but then suddenly she is huddled over herself as she pukes on my porch barely missing my feet. She takes a few breaths and then begins to apologize. "I'm so sorry."

I rake my hand through my hair as she looks at me in distress and I don't know if it's because I'm genuinely a nice guy or if it's because she looks terrible with her mascara dripping down her cheeks, but I open the front door and promptly lead her to my couch.

"I'm going to get you some water and aspirin," I shout from the kitchen as I text my brother to pick her up.

From the cabinet by the sink, I grab a glass and fill it about halfway and then pour out two aspirin into my palm from the bottle on the counter. Bailey prances toward me from the hall looking like she's ready for dinner just as I walk into the living room to find Chelsea passed out on my couch. I place both of the items on the end table by her head, and because I'm not a complete douchebag, I take a blanket from the back of the couch and drape it over her body.

"Come on, Bailey. Let's get you fed."

Four hours later I wake to incessant banging on the front door. It's so loud that even through my locked bedroom door I can hear it. Usually I sleep with it open, but I wasn't about to risk Chelsea sneaking into my room.

The knocking continues and I struggle to get out of bed and tug on a pair of sweatpants over my nude body. As I stumble down the hall, I peek into the living room and notice that Chelsea is still sleeping on my couch. Great. I would have thought Cooper would have grabbed her by now. I'm not sure how she can continue to sleep through all of the pounding on the other side of the door.

I grip the knob in my hand and twist it before yanking the door toward me.

"What do you. . .?" I begin, but the question falls from my lips as I take in Elle's neurotic state on the other side of my door.

"Please, I need you to move the car," she cries as she looks down at her tiny daughter cradled in her arms.

My heart lurches at the devastation and fear on her face, tears streaming down her cheeks in giant waves.

"I can't."

"I need to get my car. I have to take Kennedy to the ER. She's had a fever all night, and nothing is breaking it. It's at 104, Jackson. She could have a seizure. Please move your car," she pleads and out of instinct I place my hands on her shoulders drawing her attention toward me and hopefully calming her down.

"Look, I can't move the car because it's not mine. I don't know where the keys are. But I'll take you in my car. It's parked on the street. Hand me your keys and I'll grab the car seats from your vehicle, okay?"

Elle doesn't respond. Her big brown eyes look up at me in surprise and, I'm hoping, thankfulness.

"You hear me, Elle? It's going to be fine. She's going to be just fine." I try to soothe her, give her a little hope, but I can see in her eyes that until her daughter is awake and back to her cheerful self that she won't believe a word of it.

It takes a nudge of her shoulder to get her moving toward my car on the street after slipping her keys from her fingers. Once I'm inside my house I rush around frantically, my calmness while speaking to Elle completely disappearing. Though children have never been on my radar, nor am I a parent, those two little kids are freaking adorable and very polite. I hope that one day, when or if I have kids of my own, that they're just like those two.

I lurch in place as I'm mid-air at yanking down a shirt over my body.

Since when have I ever considered the thought of kids or being a parent? And why is my heart beating a million times a minute at the thought of something truly being wrong with Elle's daughter?

"Shit," I murmur into the air as I finish dressing in something more than sweatpants. I tug on a pair of sneakers and grab my keys and phone from my dresser. As I lock the front door I text my brother one last time to let him know that Chelsea is still at my house and I would really appreciate it if he or one of his fellow officers could pick her up. He replies quickly that he is on his way. An unexpected call kept him out late.

Elle's white SUV unlocks automatically as I press the button on the key fob and I grab one booster seat before skirting around to the other side to remove a harness type contraption from the other seat. The thing is massive but surprisingly lightweight.

As I approach my car, I find Elle holding her daughter closer to her face and she is singing a song softly in her ear. If time weren't so critical right now, I would think of whipping out my phone and recording it. Both her voice and the moment are beautiful and worth capturing.

"Hey," I whisper as I approach, hoping to keep her and her daughter calm. "Do you have a preference to which side to put these on?"

"Oh my God," she gasps as she looks at the carseats I carry grasped in my hands. "I forgot Noah. How could I forget Noah?" she asks frantically. "I'm a terrible mother. They're going to take away my children and give them to my ex, and he doesn't even want them," she says as her emotions begin to get the better of her. I can see her body begin to shake as she stands before me looking as if she has seen a ghost.

"It's fine, Elle. I'll get these installed real quick and run in and grab Noah. You're taking care of your daughter, and you're worried sick."

"But what if. . ." she begins, but I cut her off.

"Stop. Just get in the car, Elle."

Thankfully she nods her head and leans against the passenger side as I install both car seats. Luckily the booster goes in quickly and I latch the other in what I think is record time.

"I'll go get Noah while you strap this one in, okay?" I tell her as I'm already heading toward her house telling myself that I probably should learn her daughter's name.

I'm not sure which room is Noah's, but maybe out of instinct alone I locate a room covered in dinosaurs. In the middle of a full-size bed lies the little man clutching a T-Rex stuffed animal. Cool kid.

As I pull his covers away he immediately scrunches up his body into a ball to stave away the chill in the air. Without a second thought, I lift the tiny man into my arms and he immediately wraps himself around me, burrowing his head against my neck. Instinctively my hand goes to his back and I stroke along his spine a few times as I take in his bubblegum scent.

In all my life I have never had the overwhelming sense that I need to protect something, someone. Not since the day I saw Elle's two kids scurry into my yard asking to play with Bailey and then how I felt when I saw Elle rush over in a panic. I wanted to protect her from feeling that surge of fear, to shield her from any more wrongdoings in her life. But I can't, that isn't my place. Yet as I walk out of her home carrying Noah, I try to hide my inward smile when I consider that maybe I have it wrong, maybe it could be my place. If only she didn't make me want to pull out my own hair.

Noah stays asleep during the car ride, but Kennedy wakes up momentarily to puke all over herself and Elle, who had decided to sit in the backseat with her.

I turn into the Emergency Department area of the hospital just as Elle says, "I'm sorry for all of this trouble. I owe you, Jackson. I'll pay someone to come detail your car, and I'll get a quote for a new fence. Anything."

"Don't worry about it. It's just a car. And maybe we can talk about the fence," I add, but when I get no response I take a peek in my rearview mirror and notice that Elle's attention is on her daughter whose breathing seems to have quickened.

Thankfully I pull into an open space and Elle nimbly maneuvers her way out of the car and unlatches Kennedy all before I can place the car in park. She's halfway through the entrance when she turns toward me with a frenzied expression.

I step out of the car and say, "Don't worry, I've got Noah."

Elle nods and then proceeds to take her daughter into the ER while I carry a still sleeping Noah into the waiting room. Just as I take a seat in a quieter part of the waiting room, Noah wakes up. He groggily eyes me, glances around the room, eyes me once more with a dazed look, and then promptly falls back asleep. Ah, the life of a kid.

Taking a cue from Noah, I rest the back of my head against the wall and saddle up for a long wait ahead of me. Ten minutes later I feel the chair next to me shift and I open my eyes to find Elle in a pair of scrubs instead of her vomit-stained shorts and T-shirt staring at the blank wall ahead of us.

"Hey," I whisper, and I'm rewarded with her gaze as she steers her eyes toward me. "How is she?"

"I don't know. They said they want to give her fluids and monitor her for a while," she murmurs and then glances down to look at Noah still clutching his T-Rex. "I can take him," she says, but I clutch the boy a little tighter, not ready to give him up, and shake my head.

"It's okay, I have him. Seems like we're going to be here a while."

She sighs, "Yeah," not mentioning how I have slipped in that I'd be staying with her. She may drive me crazy but I'm not going to leave her alone in a moment like this.

"Thank you. . . for being nice to me and sorry for messing up your date," she whispers as she looks down at her hands twisting in her lap.

It's then that I remember about Chelsea. Hopefully Cooper has picked her up and she'll keep from repeating this incident again.

Needing to see Elle smile, craving it almost, I add, "No date, just someone that needed to sleep off too much alcohol. And don't worry, this is just temporary. I'm sure I'll go back to being an asshole in the morning."

Finally, I get that one puff of air, that one tiny chuckle, and all is right with the world. At least for the time being.

On a whim, I adjust Noah in my arms and use my free hand to reach out and grab one of Elle's hands. She clutches it like a lifeline and I do my freaking best to ignore the sparks shooting up my arm at her touch. It's amazing, really.

But what surprises me more is that Elle tilts to the side and rests her head on my shoulder, and everything around me floats off into oblivion. It's just me, Elle, and a five-year-old future paleontologist in my arms. If it weren't for the fact that her daughter may be fighting for her life in the other room, or that we'll both brush off this moment as happenstance, I'd say that everything feels right.

And dammit doesn't that just suck?

Chapter Five

Elle

Two Weeks Later

TURN OVER IN my bed and stare at the red illumination coming from my nightstand. Stupid alarm clock. It's been taunting me for weeks. Constantly ticking away time like I have some to spare. Every minute counts. I need at least a few hours of sleep to be able to function well, but my clock seems to have something else in mind.

"You couldn't just give me five more minutes?" I ask the inanimate object and as if it can sense my question, the number switches from a five to a six.

I groan loudly as I grab my extra pillow and try to smother myself with it. Unfortunately, it doesn't work out well for me because four minutes later my alarm sounds, alerting me to start my freaking day. As if I didn't know it already. Angrily I stare at the clock and press the snooze button, cursing it inside my head that 4 a.m. has come way too soon.

Usually I'm a morning person. I've always enjoyed waking up before the day starts and watching the sunrise while I spend a few hours baking. My kids are sound sleepers so it has always been my personal private time.

But two weeks ago everything changed. The night I had to rush Kennedy to the emergency room for a fever that medicine couldn't break, my world changed. Jackson, my irritating, asshole of a neighbor came to my rescue. He drove us to the hospital, not complaining once as Kennedy vomited all over his clean interior (and me!) or as he held a sleeping Noah in his arms in the most uncomfortable chairs known to man. Someone really ought to tell healthcare providers that all waiting rooms are uncomfortable.

But what really changed for me that night, or early morning considering it was around 3 a.m., was that he held me. It was just for comfort and consolation, but the way his hand wrapped around my much smaller one and the way he gently rubbed circles across the back had put me under a spell.

And I want it broken – now.

I can't sleep. Every night when I close my eyes, he's there. Jackson is there waiting for me in that space between darkness and consciousness. He's waiting with all of his sexiness: the tattoos, unruly dark hair, and lean muscles that I want to trace with my tongue. And that's the problem. Ever since that moment when he showed just an ounce of empathy I was lost, hypnotized, and I hate every second of it.

I don't want to feel this way again. I feel like I'm trapped under someone's spell and I can't break free. That was how it began with Dan. He spun a web that I couldn't free myself from until it was too late and he had found a new plaything. I was lost in Dan and our marriage. My only outlet was my baking, and when my world fell apart, I clung to it with everything I had.

And now? Now that I can't stop thinking about my exasperating neighbor my baking sucks. I've screwed up three recipes in the past two weeks. Simple mistakes that I should never be making at this point. Because who still mixes up salt and sugar? Not this baker. I never even made that mistake when I was learning from my grandmother.

Add in the fact that I haven't seen Jackson since he brought us home from the hospital and my mind is a wreck. I'm torn in two. I'm torn between wanting him and hating him. Craving a glimpse of him and wishing I could get over my new infatuation.

"Come on, Elle. Give it up," I whisper into my empty room just as my five-minute snooze goes off.

Knowing that I have a large order to work on this morning, I swing my legs over the side of the bed. Just as my foot drops onto the floor, I hear loud grumbling sounds from outside my window.

"Are you kidding me?" I say to no one as I peek through my large pane window and find no one there.

Mumbling, I throw open my bedroom door paying little mind to the fact that I'm heading outside wearing a silk camisole and shorts.

I notice a man with a weed eater standing in my ditch swiping the machine back and forth as it cuts the grass. It's not the same man from two weeks ago. He was blond and much younger. I watch slack-jawed as the muscles of the shirtless man bunch around his shoulders. His forearms are tight and corded, and his veins pulse with the movements of the machine. And I never knew it before, but apparently, I am extremely turned on by forearms – not just Dan's. I feel my panties dampen as he works the tool, his bottom tightening with each step. I'm also turned on by a nice butt. But I'm pretty sure all women are.

It's only 4 a.m. but sweat beads along my hairline and around my clavicle as I watch the man trim my yard. Maybe this is the guy that can break the spell Jackson has me under. Maybe this one will solve my problem.

But as he turns to the side, I take a good look at his arms and find one covered in a full sleeve of tattoos. The same tattoos that grace Jackson's perfect arms. I inhale a quick breath as I realize my error.

With my hand on my neck, I try to walk slowly back into the house to not draw attention to myself, but as if he can sense me from afar, his perfect face turns toward me in surprise. My chance to hide is gone, so I stand there awkwardly and use my free hand to send a small wave in his direction. Right off my thigh. Like a middle schooler seeing her crush in the mall. Awkward.

I expect him to continue working, so I'm equally as surprised when he cuts off the machine, frees two plugs from his ears, and begins to stalk toward me. Of course, I can't help but watch his chest as he saunters toward me looking like he's taking a stroll down a fashion runway. He definitely missed his calling. With his jawline and blue eyes, he would have made it far in that world.

"Hey," he calls out as he gets closer and I have to force myself to speak in return.

Of course, I can't form an actual civilized sentence. Something like, "Hey, I'm surprised to see you," or something like that. No. Instead I spout out, "What are you doing mowing my yard at four in the morning?" Because apparently, I'm that kid in kindergarten that was mean to the other kid that they liked.

Jackson halts and then looks at me confused before running one of his magnificent fingers through his hair.

"Sorry, I'm covering some for my cousin. He's sick. I have a lot of lawns to take care of today. Didn't think you'd mind," he adds smugly.

On instinct my hands go straight to my hips, balling themselves into fists.

"Well, I do mind. I have work to do and I can't concentrate." I leave out the fact that my concentration has little to do with the noise but more to do with the man himself.

"Look, Elle. I'm sorry, but I don't really have a choice. My next opening isn't for two days and I'd really just like to get this done. And I promise this will be the last time. I have two new hires starting next week."

"New hires? I thought you owned the gym," I ask puzzled.

"Yeah, I happen to own two businesses. Sorry if that surprises you. I co-own this one with my cousin." I open my mouth to apologize for sounding like a stuck-up brat but Jackson quickly tacks on, "Now, if you don't mind, I'm going to get back to work. You can probably fit in a nap later, princess."

My mouth hangs open for a different reason this time, and as I work up my retaliation at the nickname, Jackson stuffs his earplugs back into his ears and walks back toward the weed eater sitting in the ditch.

I would give anything to march right up to him and give him a piece of my mind, but instead, I take another minute to ogle him before turning around and heading inside. Might as well start my day.

It's awful. All of it. I can't even make a pound cake that doesn't taste like something the kids would have concocted.

"Mommy, why are you throwing out another cake? I want to eat the yummies," Kennedy says from her perch at the table as she nibbles on some cereal.

"I'm sure you would but it didn't taste very good, sweetie. If I make one that tastes yummy I'll share it with you."

"Everything you make tastes yummy, Mommy," Noah chimes in and damn if that doesn't just melt my heart. I could probably feed my kids scrapings from a pot and they would eat it. They do snack on chalk, glue sticks, and slime. . .because kids. Which probably doesn't say much about my baking skills.

"You're sweet my little munchkin. Mommy is going to take a quick shower and then try this again. Now, what did we talk about?"

"No going outside."

"Correct," I say as I tap the tip of their noses with my index fingers covered in flour. "I'll be right back."

"Okay, Mommy," the kids reply as they both focus in on their electronic tablets.

After wiping my hands on a dish towel, I make my way toward my bathroom, my need for a shower almost overwhelming me. Since my run-in with Jackson this morning, my skin has felt heated and overly sensitive. The silk of my camisole and shorts scrape against my skin and I have to stifle a gasp at the sensation. The coolness of the material against my warmth is almost shocking, but as I step under the pulsating spray of my shower, I realize my grave mistake. The water feels like tiny prickles all over my body; nips and pinches that run borderline between pain and pleasure.

I lean my head back allowing the water to trickle down my neck, across my stomach, and between my legs. One of the streams of spray hits the bundle of nerves between my legs and my hand juts out to grasp the tiled wall. Bliss pours from my body with every vibration of the water on my clit. Closing my eyes, I try to picture Chris Hemsworth or Chris Evans. Hell, right now I'd take any of the *Avengers,* but my mind instantly goes to my sexy as sin neighbor. The way his body moved in the early morning light. How even at the premature hour the sweat poured down his body. Sweat I wanted to lap with my tongue to see if he tasted sweet or salty.

What would he look like having sex? Would he exert as much energy to please a woman? Would his body move the same way?

I begin to imagine his fingers trailing the same path on my body as the water. His hands would sliver down my neck, the tips of his fingers tracing the delicate skin of my collarbone. They would then caress my breast testing their weight and rolling my nipples between his thumb and forefinger, the feeling sending waves of pleasure to my core. Jackson's mouth would join in on the exploration, his tongue needing a taste of the tight peaks as his hands trail down my stomach and hips to their destination between my legs. Almost as if he is there with me, I slide a finger across my center, reveling in the warmth exuding from my sex. Using my thumb, I gently run circles around my exposed clit as the water pulses against it.

My orgasm comes quickly, almost shocking me back into reality. The bathroom is heavy with mist from the heat of my shower, and I cringe as I consider how long I must have been in here.

On wobbly legs, I leave the shower and wrap myself in a towel. Peeking out from the door I'm relieved to find my kids still sitting like little angels at the table, both entranced with their devices. Thank goodness for small miracles.

In my bedroom, I toss on my business attire consisting of a T-shirt and a pair of shorts. After my personal tryst in the shower, I feel a bit more relaxed, not so wound up. Maybe giving in to my desire for Jackson is what I needed. I usually try to ignore that I want him. That I want to feel him inside of me. But this morning I didn't stop it. I let the thoughts and sensations run wild.

With my newfound energy, I step into my kitchen and ask the kids to go outside and play before the day gets hot, reminding them that they need to stay in our yard and not to venture over to Jackson's. Luckily I learned that Bailey is his brother's dog and he was only dog-sitting, so I won't have to worry about the kids bothering him.

I look over three orders I need to finish, all simple recipes I've done over a hundred times. A batch of twenty miniature pound cakes, strawberry cupcakes, and a pineapple upside down cake. Easy peasy. Should be at least, but all were a disaster this morning, and I hate when I have to waste good ingredients. I also need to test out my recipe for Kennedy's birthday cake for next weekend.

My little princess will be turning four. Of course, it's also the weekend before Noah starts kindergarten. Everything is changing around me and I'm just. . . here. Stuck in this little safe world I've crafted for myself. A place where I can't get hurt.

Three hours later I'm staring at my creations with a zealous smile on my face. They're all complete and they're all delicious. Finally. Maybe giving into my thoughts on Jackson was exactly what I needed.

Stepping outside, I watch Noah push Kennedy on the swing and my heart soars. This is all I need. If all I'm given are dirty thoughts about Jackson to make my baking the best it can be then I'll take it, because everything in my life should revolve around my kids.

A few minutes later I join the kids in their clubhouse and we have a makeshift tea party, which Noah protects with his soldier action figures. I hear my name being called from the house and I realize that Sara is paying us an unexpected visit. We haven't seen her since dinner about two weeks ago.

"Hey, we're out here!" I shout as she steps onto the back deck.

Sara walks over to us as I am making my way down the ladder.

"Guys, y'all play nice. I'm going to chat with Miss Sara, okay?"

"Yes, Mommy," they reply, and I smile up at them from their lair.

"Hey, what an unexpected surprise," I say to Sara as we exchange a hug.

"Hey. So, can we talk?" she asks with a solemn expression, and I instantly know that whatever she has to say is not good.

"Yeah."

I guide her into the house and we take a seat at the kitchen table, me facing the yard so I can still watch the kids.

"Elle, this is important," Sara says, which immediately gets my attention, and by her expression I know that whatever she has to say is going to change everything.

"What's up?"

"So, you know how part of the divorce agreement is that Dan needed to continue to carry both children on his insurance?"

Dread begins to fill me as I nod in understanding.

"Well, the court received communication from the insurance company that he has taken the liberty to remove coverage for Noah and Kennedy. Apparently, he didn't realize that the court would be made privy to his decision. Idiot."

"Why didn't the hospital say anything when they ran the card? They had me pay the coinsurance."

"I don't know. Most of that information is printed on the card and some hospitals don't run insurance for billing until after."

"Sara, what am I going to do? I can only afford insurance for myself and I won't be able to add the kids with the way my business is going right now."

"Well, first and foremost, the judge is going to make sure that Dan reinstates the insurance or he is going to have to pay you whatever your coverage for them would be. But that means we're going to have to go back to court."

"Court?" God, I'm so tired of court. All I want is for all of this to be over. All I want is Dan out of my life.

"I'm so sorry, Elle. I don't know why he is doing this."

I snake my hands through my hair in exasperation. "He's doing this because he wants to torment me. This means he has to stay in my life. It was bad enough I had to invite him to Kennedy's party next weekend. I can promise you that he and his family want nothing to do with me and the kids."

"I wish I had better news."

"It's not your fault. I guess I know what I'll be doing this afternoon."

Sara leaves a little after lunch, having ordered sandwiches for all of us. As we ate, Kennedy told her all about the unicorn party she's having next week. I had wanted to set her up with a unicorn photo session I had seen one day scrolling through social media, but after seeing the price tag, I realized that I wouldn't be able to afford it. Hell, I can't even afford to do a regular photo shoot. Keeping the utilities covered is taking about everything in my bank account. My trust was pretty much drained in the divorce, just a little backup savings for an emergency sits there now.

Leaving the kids in their rooms for quiet time, Noah reading a book and Kennedy watching a learning video, I go to check the mail, hoping for a glimpse of Jackson to brighten my day but I'm not so lucky. As I pull the envelopes from the mailbox, I realize that I must be one of the unluckiest people on earth.

A bill from the hospital sits heavy in my hand. I should have expected it; I'm not sure why I haven't. I go inside and tear through the envelope. When I see the amount I drop the bill on the table as if it will scald me. A bill for over thirty-five thousand dollars glares back at me as if expecting a response.

"Hey, Mommy," a soft voice calls out from the hallway. "Can you read me a book?" Kennedy asks rubbing her eyes. My brave little girl who had some sort of infection and is finally finished with her medication from her visit to the Emergency Department.

"Sure." I smile warmly at her. How I'm going to pay the bill, I'm not sure, but I am sure that I can shower my kids with all the love that I have. All that Dan hasn't destroyed.

Sitting at the kitchen table under a single pendant light, I feel like the stereotypical single parent wondering how they're going to make ends meet. The kids had begged and pleaded for another book at bedtime and I caved. I couldn't deny them anything tonight. Now they're both safely tucked into their beds and the sun ducks itself behind the night sky as evening falls around my house.

I don't hear the cicadas buzzing outside or the birds whistling their goodnights. All I hear is the pounding in my ears as I stare at the hospital invoice. I had texted Sara earlier and asked her what I needed to do, but she wasn't sure. I have the option of waiting until a judge has Dan reinstate the insurance, but that doesn't mean the insurance will accept the service date. I can contact the hospital and ask for a payment plan, but because of my available income, they may deny it. So I can either pay now or hold out hope that the judge and the insurance company will rectify the situation.

Scattering the papers from the divorce, the bill, and my current bank statements across the table, I finally give in to my emotions. With my elbows on the table, I rest my face in the palms of my hands and let the devastating sobs control me. I can feel each break, each wave of sorrow rush through me. My body shakes and lurches with each gasp of air.

"Elle?" I hear from behind me, and I quickly turn in surprise to find Jackson standing inside my sliding glass door with an alarmed look on his face. I try to wipe away the tears that have soaked my face, but I know that it's no use trying to disguise my emotions. Dan always said I was an ugly crier and my skin turned the color of a tomato when I was upset.

"Sorry, the door was unlocked. I have the invoice for the lawn," he explains as he holds out a printed invoice. "I figured it was easier this way than mailing it. Being neighbors and all," he jokes, trying to lighten the mood but I stare at the paper like it's going to give me a disease. "Are you okay?"

That question gets my attention.

Looking at Jackson, I ask cynically, "Am I okay? Let me ask you something, Jackson. Have you ever been divorced?"

He steps into the kitchen fully,and as he tugs one of the chairs closer to me to sit down, he says, "No. Can't say that I have."

"Well, it sucks. Especially when he wants everything of mine but his own kids. It doesn't matter that the judge requires visitation and for him to cover them on his insurance. Now I'm stuck with this god awful bill and no way to pay it," I cry out hysterically as I shove the bill toward him and explain everything Sara mentioned earlier. "They're gonna come take my kids away from me because I'm a terrible mother and I can't take care of them."

I hide behind my hands once more as I allow my tears to fall. Hot, heavy tears of despair. I don't notice that his eyes widen at the size of the bill from the hospital or that he grabs a box of tissues from the countertop by the sink.

"Hey," he says kindly, and I look over at him as he holds the box in my direction. Snagging a tissue, I wipe at my face, wondering how awful I must look to him or whether he thinks I'm a crazy person. With my luck, he'll probably put his house on the market tomorrow.

"I can help you with this bill, Elle."

"What?" I whisper because I have clearly misheard him.

"It's not your fault that you assumed your kids were insured. I can pay the bill for you while you wait for the court to figure out this shit with your ex. And when the insurance figures it all out, you can pay me back. It's no big deal."

"Are you serious right now? It is a big deal. That's a lot of freaking money, Jackson. And you hate me, remember?"

"It's really not. I have two businesses. I make pretty decent money and I barely spend any of it. And I don't hate you," he says warmly as he brushes back a few loose strands of my hair and tucks them behind my ear.

"I can sell you a car," I blurt out unexpectedly, surprising both Jackson and myself.

"I don't need your car. And clearly, you do," he replies as he gazes at me with a strange look.

"No, I have a classic, fully restored Mustang. It was a gift from my grandfather. It's all I have left of him. I can sell it to you. I'm sure it's worth at least half of what I would owe you. You can do whatever you want with it."

"I'm not taking the car, Elle."

"Let me give you something. Anything. Please," I plead.

"Kiss me."

Well, that is not what I was expecting to hear. Surprised, I look over at him and search his eyes, shocked to find sincerity and something akin to desire swirling in his irises.

"You want a kiss. . .from me. . .in exchange for paying my hospital bill? At least until I can pay you back. Seems kind of one-sided," I mumble.

He leans in closer, and my nose fills with his overwhelming scent, and at that moment I almost wish that he had asked for more than just a kiss.

"Kiss me, Elle," he demands as his nose brushes against mine and I'm lost. So lost in the thought of pressing my lips against his and running my fingers through his hair that I don't realize he's pulled me even closer, our breath mingling in the small space between us.

Closing my eyes, I lean that inch closer pressing my mouth against his. We stay like that for a moment, an innocent peck between two acquaintances, but then the air shifts. Jackson tilts his head slightly and his lips brush across mine at the same time his hand twines itself in my hair causing a gasp to escape between my lips.

As my mouth opens, Jackson's tongue sneaks past the opening and grazes against my own. The touch is minuscule but it erupts something inside of me.

Without hesitation I reach out and place my hands on Jackson's shoulders, running them down his biceps and around to his back. He shifts his body, bringing himself impossibly closer as he wraps an arm around my waist and tugs me onto his lap effortlessly.

God, how long has it been since I've been held this way? Desired this way? Months? Years? All I know is that at this moment I have never felt as coveted as I do right now.

Our kiss goes on for minutes, remarkable moments in time that electrify my body. I want more, need more, but a small cry from down the hall has us pulling apart in surprise, both of us needing a second to remember where we are. Who we are.

"Mommy?" the soft voice beckons from her room drawing my attention as Jackson quietly deposits me back onto my chair.

I turn my attention back to him for a moment to ask what all of this means. He stands by the sliding glass door, hand poised on the handle.

"Elle, you're worth every penny," he adds, before he slides out of my house and back into the oblivion.

If I couldn't still taste him on my lips or feel his hands on my skin, I'd think he was a figment of my imagination.

"Mommy," Kennedy cries out again, but I find myself staring off into the darkened sky wondering what to do now.

Damn that Jackson and his amazing kisses.

Chapter Six

Jackson

I DIDN'T SLEEP WORTH shit last night. After having my first taste of Elle, I had to physically force myself to pull away from her. Or else I was going to drag her to the first solid surface I could find and ravage every inch of her body. She was as sweet as I had imagined and I want more.

I watch as my parents pull their car in front of the house, parking on the street as I had requested. Elle and I haven't had any more run-ins regarding the driveway, but I'm sure it's coming. Truthfully we should just go in together and have it widened to accommodate both vehicles, but that would require having to have a civilized conversation.

Today my parents are coming by for our monthly cookout. My brother and I swap turns every two weeks and this week it's mine. But I love to cook and grill, so I'm always glad when it's my turn.

Unfortunately, I know that my mom will be peppering me for details about Elle. Ever since she saw her and the kids leave my yard a few weeks ago, she's been asking about my new neighbor.

Grabbing the steaks, I go ahead and walk out to my deck knowing my parents will make themselves comfortable in the house. Outside, the laughter of my neighbors catch my attention and I watch as Noah pushes Kennedy on her swing, the girl laughing wildly as she pumps her legs to go higher.

Noah must sense me because he turns around and waves frantically before helping Kennedy come to a stop. They rush toward me and though I want to hate that they're here in my yard and as much as I know Elle will be unhappy about it, I secretly welcome their intrusion. Their tiny faces light up as I wave them over and they eagerly bounce on their toes as they watch me open the top of the grill.

Kennedy tries to get a closer look, one of her brown curls almost falling over the grill slats as she pushes a chair and climbs on top.

"Hey guys, this has fire, and fire hurts so let's stay back, okay?"

"Okay, Mister Jackson," they say in unison. Noah helps Kennedy move the chair back some and then they both look at me in fascination.

I can sense her approach before I hear her. As I place the first steak on the grill, it's not the sizzle of the meat that I hear, it's her soft laugh as Kennedy calls out to her.

"Mommy, we're watching Mister Jackson make meat."

"Well, that must be very interesting. I have the lemonade you both asked for. Why don't you have a seat on your bottoms so you can drink it?"

"Okay, Mommy," they both reply as they scurry down to the steps and have a seat, Elle handing them each a closed cup with a straw.

I place the rest of the steaks on the grill as she walks over to me and I secretly wonder how awkward our conversation is going to go. It's easier when the kids can act as a distraction.

"Hey, sorry if they're bothering you," she starts as she steps up next to me at the grill.

I close the lid and toss the tongs on the plate resting on the attached stand and turn toward her. My eyes skim over her, feasting on every delectable ounce of exposed skin. The skin I want to taste inch by inch. Finally, I make it to her face, quickly bypassing her shorts and T-shirt, and notice the small smirk of her mouth. Clearly she noticed my perusal and I'm not even ashamed.

"They're fine. I don't mind them watching."

"Do you cook a lot?" she asks as the sliding glass doors open and my dad steps out with two beers in hand.

He hands me a bottle as I say, "I do. I enjoy cooking actually. This is my dad, Stan. Dad, this is my neighbor Elle and her two kids Noah and Kennedy."

The munchkins wave from their perch on the steps before taking another sip of their drinks.

Elle holds her hand out to my dad and he accepts it warmly.

"Nice to meet you, Elle. Are you staying for dinner?"

"Um. . ." she hums as I add, "I'm not sure that I have enough steaks, Dad."

"Oh, your brother messaged me and he won't be able to make it. He got called in last minute. Some drug case going on across town. Why don't you join us, Elle? It would be silly to let this food go to waste."

I watch in fascination as Elle rocks back and forth on her feet, just slight movements. Not enough to call attention, but if you're paying her any mind you can notice it along with the slight blush of her cheeks.

"I wouldn't want to impose," she whispers as she bites the corner of her bottom lip.

If my dad weren't here with us right now that move alone would have me dragging her inside, caveman style.

"You're not an imposition, Elle." My voice is deep, gravely, my desire for Elle laced in every syllable.

Elle stares at me for a beat, gauging my words and their truth, then takes a peek at her kids before nodding and accepting the invitation.

"Please don't go through any trouble. The kids and I aren't picky eaters, we can share whatever you have."

"There will be plenty. Don't you worry," my dad assures us as he pats her shoulder gently, already falling under her spell.

Welcome to the club.

"Oh!" she shouts, startling us as I begin to open the grill to flip the steaks. The top clangs loudly as I quickly close it.

"Sorry," she winces. "I can bring dessert. It's not much, but I promise that it's delicious."

"Elle, you don't have to-"

"Please, I want to. I'll be right back."

I watch her scurry across the yard again, the shorts wrapped around her bottom tugging with every step and I have to work at hiding my erection behind my pants. Noticing Noah and Kennedy sitting on the steps, my dad begins chatting with them and they beam as he asks them about their playset and the newest kids television show.

I don't even know how he knows this crap.

"Why don't you guys go inside with my dad and help set the table?"

"Go inside?" one of them asks while the other asks, "Is Bailey inside?"

"No, Bailey is with my brother. She is his dog." Their smiles turn into frowns when I mention that Bailey isn't with me, but I quickly perk them up at the mention of my mom. "But my mom is inside and she gives really good hugs. And I hear she has superpowers and can tell you if you're a princess or a superhero."

Kennedy's big blue widen as she gasps, "Can she tell if I am a superhero princess?"

"You betcha."

"Wow."

As I finally flip the steaks, my dad opens the sliding glass doors ushering the kids inside where my mom greets them warmly, and with hugs, which are definitely her specialty.

"You're good with them," my dad says, his opposing body leaning against the doorframe.

"They're easy and they're good kids."

"How often are you around them?"

"Um. . . twice?"

My dad cocks one of his eyebrows in a silent response and I shrug my shoulders.

"I like her too," he continues, and I nod because I know what he's implying. They've been pestering about grandkids for years and here lies a perfectly set up family dropped into my lap.

But I'm not ready for that. A family isn't something I've ever had on my horizon. An equal balance of work and play is what I'm cut out for.

Except as my dad steps inside the house, just as Elle steps out of hers with a container in her hands, I can't help but wonder if my plans have some wiggle room.

"Hey," she announces as she steps back onto the deck, her smile instantly illuminating the area in her light. "I brought a pineapple upside-down cake."

"Sounds delicious," I respond, peering into my kitchen through the glass and am relieved to find no one in my line of sight. Without hesitation, I reach out and wrap an arm around Elle's small frame, yanking her against me. She moves willingly as if she is anticipating the move.

I seal our lips together, a hungry kiss of eagerness and longing, of want and desire. Her tongue peeks out tentatively tasting my lips, and I accept her intrusion, matching it with my own inquisition. My grip tightens on her waist and at that moment I wish that we were anywhere else but outside. It's not that I don't want to have sex with Elle, believe me, I do, but I just want – her. I crave her taste, her touch. It's addictive.

She pulls back an inch and gazes up at me with innocence in her eyes, a guileless expression.

"I wasn't positive if last night was a dream or not," she whispers, and I have to smile because it felt like a dream for me too. "Or if we were going to talk about it."

"Oh, it definitely wasn't a dream. And I hope there will be little talking next time."

"Next time?" she questions with that same innocent expression, and I have to hold back my laugh.

"Oh, there will definitely be a next time. And with a lot fewer clothes." She swallows hard, the movement of her throat significant. And as if my mom has a sixth sense, she steps out onto the deck and saves me from the retreat Elle is contemplating. It's written all over her face.

"Hi, honey. Are the steaks almost ready?"

"Yes, Mom. And this is Elle. Why don't you show her inside?"

"Oh, I'd love to. You can call me Naomi. Your two kids are the sweetest things ever," my mom claims as they step inside leaving me to my thoughts.

Yes, there will definitely be fewer clothes next time.

Noah and Kennedy kept us occupied during dinner, each of them taking turns telling us a story about slaying a dragon and a princess falling in love with a beast. I missed the details, but my parents and Elle were riveted. My attention was solely on Elle, her eyes lighting up every time one of the kids got excited about something in the story. It was fascinating.

Now she, my mom, and Kennedy are serving the pieces of cake on plates I never knew I had.

"This is a new recipe, so tell me what you think," Elle says as she places the cake in front of me before taking her own seat. "The kids love it, but they may be a bit biased."

I take a bite along with my mom and dad and we all seem to groan in unison. The cake appears to be laced with the flavor of pineapple and brown sugar with hints of cinnamon catching on my taste buds.

"This is incredible." My parents praise Elle as they take another bite, but I can sense Elle's attention remains on me waiting for my response to her concoction.

"What do you think?" she whispers, and I can hear the fear of rejection in her voice.

Turning toward her I pin her with my gaze making sure she hears every word. "Elle, this is amazing. You have a gift."

"Thank you. I may not be a great cook, but I'm a decent baker. That's my business. I do online and local orders. A few of the restaurants in town carry my items."

Her smile widens as she notices my surprise. I had no idea she ran a baking business out of her home. First, it's ingenious. Second, it makes perfect sense.

"Wow," I reply as I take another hearty bite of the cake, savoring its flavor.

"Tell us more about your business," my mother says, and Elle dives into how she wants to expand and sell her recipes to bakeries and place the items in her name. She has a few contracts she has bid on for some well-known restaurants. I listen intently as she explains that during her divorce the judge questioned how she could make a living doing online baking orders but when he saw her receipts, and she named off restaurants that she currently supplies desserts to, the judge seemed appeased. Which means Elle knows what she is doing.

Taking a final bite of my cake, a bit disheartened that I've finished the dessert, I suggest, "If you ever need help with the business side, I'd be happy to help."

"Really?" she asks, shocked at my offer. "I actually do have a few questions about contracts and invoicing if you have a chance to talk about it sometime."

"Sure. You know where to find me," I imply, and she blushes at my hidden meaning. I also catch the knowing grins on my parents' faces. In their heads they've probably both married us off and added a few more kids to Elle's brood.

"Well, kids, we're going to head out. Elle, thank you for joining us tonight. It has been a pleasure to get to know you and your adorable children," my mother says as she hugs Elle, Noah, and Kennedy. The kids' tiny arms wrap around my mom's waist as if they've known her for years. Elle does the same.

As my mom reaches me, she grips my shoulders tight as she pulls me close. "Don't screw this up, Jackson. I like her."

"Mom," I groan, but she simply kisses my cheek and tells me that she loves me.

"Love you too."

I stand at the front door watching my parents get into their car and pull out, then I turn to Elle who is busying herself trying to clean up the mess from dinner.

"I'll do that. You don't need to clean."

"Oh, it's no problem. You cooked."

"Elle," I command, and she drops the sponge back into the sink filled with soapy water. "Thank you for dessert. It was delicious," I confess as I move through the house stepping closer to her. She leans against the kitchen counter waiting for me to approach but her eyes are wild, flicking back and forth between me and her kids. I can see the fear there. The fear of what her kids will perceive. They've only been away from their father for a month.

I come to stand up against her, my hands on either side of her on the counter, boxing her in. Her breath quickens, coming in heavy pants as she rests her hands on my chest, neither pushing me away or pulling me in.

"Jackson, I'm not sure-"

"Why don't you and the kids head back home?"

"Yeah," she whispers. "That's a good idea. They need a bath."

Stroking my hand through her hair, letting the silk strands fall between each finger, I ask, "I'll see you later?"

"Sure."

In a daze she gathers up Noah and Kennedy and steps across the yard back to their home. I watch as they travel inside, and just as I think she's shut the door, Elle peeks the upper part of her body back outside and waves. Even from this distance, I can see the smile on her face.

Yeah, I should think about making room for a family.

It's dark in my room, the only light filtering in through my window being that from the full moon outside. I have the window open, the night air cool and crisp, but not cold enough to cause a chill. It's perfect sleeping weather.

But I can't sleep, it's another night with insomnia. Another night with Elle on my mind. I could see it in her today too, she hasn't been sleeping. She tried to mask it, but the bags were evident beneath her eyes.

Gazing out my window that faces the yard, I'm hoping that she's at least getting a little shut-eye tonight. Maybe my help alleviated some of her stress. Kissing her was a small price for what she needed, but I would offer millions for more of her kisses. They are that potent. That drug-inducing.

I can see the clock against the wall and notice that it is just past midnight. I have to open the gym tomorrow for my yoga class, so I groan as I toss the sheets from my bed and head into the kitchen. A glass of milk is something my mom always gave me growing up when I couldn't sleep, and I'm hoping that it works the same tonight.

I pour a large glass and take a sip, letting the cool soothing drink trickle down my throat. Out the sliding glass doors, I watch as an owl perches on top of a fence post and hoots into the air, his body shadowed by the moonlight. As if he is beckoning me, I step through the doors after opening them and move onto the deck.

It's like a different world outside, everything is a different shade of blue in the light cast by the moon. It's almost seductive in the way it masks you in its shadows.

For some unexplained reason, I peer over at Elle's house. I wonder if she is awake. If she can't sleep like me. If she is thinking about our kiss from earlier. If she imagines me kissing her again. Or is she still crying, fretting over that ridiculous hospital bill.

I hate seeing women cry, it breaks something inside me. My mom always said I was an empathetic child; if she cried I would cry. It seems to have carried itself over to adulthood. Maybe that's why I'm a great personal trainer. I can empathize with my member's struggles, understand their pain and journey.

I'm not sure what calls to me, but before I know it I've set my empty glass of milk aside and wandered over to Elle's house. I'm not quite sure which window is hers, but I assume the layout is the same as mine. I notice a large picture window facing the backyard and the curtains are swept aside, one of the windows is open letting in the breeze.

If I didn't know that this is a safe neighborhood I would scold her for leaving herself vulnerable like this. Hell, I'll probably still scold her.

She looks beautiful in the light, her room colored in grays and whites. Her body faces away from me and it's covered in a pale sheet. I'm staring at her through the window like a Peeping Tom, but I can't help myself.

"How long are you going to stare?" she asks as she turns over with a smile on her face.

If I were a lesser man I would be shrieking into the night but this girl. . . she knows I am being pulled toward her and I end up laughing.

"Figured you'd make me climb through a window like a high schooler," I say as I pull myself through the window landing with a soft thud on the rug covering her hardwood floors, thankful there was no screen to remove.

I inspect her room a little further and she watches in amusement. Her exterior wall is covered in white painted brick and the headboard of her bed rests against it. She has hung a few pictures, but other than that and a dresser across the way, her room is decorated minimally. I assume it's because she spent her effort decorating her kids' rooms. But truthfully this room is a reflection of her. Simple, clean, a hidden beauty.

"I like your room," I say as I take a step closer to her.

"Thanks," she replies, and I can imagine the slight blush that is rushing on her cheeks.

Her pink tongue slips between her lips, coating them in moisture, and they immediately draw my attention. I'm spellbound. Without vacillation, I prop one knee onto her bed and then the other. As I crawl toward her, she pushes her sheet away exposing her body covered in the same outfit from the other morning. A color that almost matches her porcelain skin.

I don't move on top of her as she probably expects, but I lie beside her, forcing her to turn her body toward me. One arm bends at the elbow and I prop up my head so I'm looking down at her slightly and my other hand reaches out and rests against her waist. I massage the material covering her body and then slip underneath to stroke her soft skin.

I want to explore her and I will, but now at this very moment, I want to taste her again. I need to get my hit. Using my strength, I tug her the remaining distance, that minimal twelve inches between us, and cradle her body against mine.

"Are you going to kiss me now?" she asks, and I find myself chuckling again. This girl has me laughing more in the past two days than I have in weeks, months.

"Is that what you've been waiting for?" I reply as I trail my hand up toward her breast, the tip of my finger stroking against the skin on the side and then moving back down to rest on her waist.

"It's all I've been thinking about," she admits shyly, her teeth nibbling at her bottom lip.

Tilting my head toward her, I watch as she closes her eyes in anticipation of my kiss. Instead, I tease her by brushing my lips against the corner of her mouth and then pressing a kiss to her jawline. "Tell me. Tell me what you've been thinking about."

As I continue kissing every angle of her jaw and her face she says, "I've been thinking about how perfect your lips felt against mine. How you tasted. How I have never been kissed like that before."

"And how is that?" I ask as I kiss her closed eyelids, smirking when a soft sigh escapes between her lips.

"Like it was a fairytale. Like the world stopped. Time stood still. The everything blurred around me."

"Really?" I ask pulling back. I'm impressed that she dared to admit how she felt during our kiss. I'm even more surprised that she feels the same as I do. I don't want to admit that this could be the start of something more. I'm not that inexperienced in relationships to think that a kiss is the foundation for a relationship. But with Elle, it sure feels that way.

"I'm sorry. Does that freak you out?" Elle doesn't look embarrassed by her proclamation and I guess that's because she has nothing to lose by it.

"It should," I admit, "but it doesn't."

Moving my hand from her waist I snake it into her hair, tightening my fingers into a fist as I pull her head toward me. Her eyes close again and I join her as I seal our lips together. And just as they have the past two times, the world and all of my worries fall away. Elle weaves me into her fantasy and I can't pull free. Not that I want to. I've never wanted to be lost in a fairytale more than right at this moment.

She moans into my mouth and rocks against me as our tongues weave and explore each other's mouths, taking turns in their journey. Without refrain, I pull my hand free from her hair and stroke down her back until I find one of the succulent globes of her bottom, the ass I have been admiring since she moved in more than a month ago. With zero preamble, I squeeze the rounded globe as I slide one of my legs between hers. She's rocking against me like a teenager getting off for the first time. I haven't dry humped in years, the women I'm with usually go straight toward the end game, but not Elle. She's going to take me for everything I'm worth. And I don't give a damn at all.

Against my leg I can feel her wetness growing, seeping through her panties and silk shorts. It's a heady feeling knowing that I can do this to her, for her.

"Jackson," she moans as I let my hand slip between her legs from behind.

"You like that?" I ask, even though I already know the answer.

"Yes," she replies breathlessly. One of her hands slips across my bare chest feeling my muscles quiver under her touch and I have to stifle back my growl.

Suddenly I have the strong desire to taste her, to see if she is as sweet as those concoctions she creates. I use my strength to roll her onto her back and I slip down her body tugging her shorts and panties with me.

"I want to kiss you," I proclaim as I hold up one of her feet, her ankle a few inches from my mouth.

"I thought you were kissing me," she jests, and I smile in return.

"I want to kiss you here," I say as I place a kiss on her ankle and then move a bit higher on her leg and add, "And here."

I continue my path until I'm so close to her center that I can smell her heat, then I move to the other leg and repeat the motion. I watch in fascination as her hands begin to grip the bed as I continue to move closer and closer to her apex.

Finally, I place a soft kiss on her bare mound and my name is nothing more than a breath from her lips. I run my nose against her clit and she stills as if no man has ventured to this part of her before. But that can't be, right? She's gorgeous. Any man in his right mind would be praying that she let him go down on her like this. I know I feel honored to have the privilege.

"You smell amazing," I say reverently, tracing one of my fingers through her folds, her body still remaining frozen beneath me.

"Relax, Elle. I'm going to make you feel good."

"I've never. No one has ever-" she trails off, her embarrassment palpable in the room.

"Hey, I can stop if you're uncomfortable," I explain, even though that is the last thing I want to do.

"No," she rushes out. "Please don't stop. It's just. . . new, that's all."

I run my finger through her slick folds again and she shivers beneath my touch. "Does it feel good?"

"Yes," she gasps as I circle her clit peeking out from behind its hood.

I remove my fingers and wait for her attention to fall on me before I lick my fingers clean as she watches. A growl escapes from deep in my chest as her flavor lands on my tongue, the perfect combination of sweet and salty, just like I had imagined.

"Your ex is an idiot if he never put his mouth on you. You're delectable. And I'm not just saying that."

"Mmm," she murmurs as I lean back down and slip my tongue against her sex.

I continue to lick and savor her flavor until her legs quake beneath my hands.

"Are you close, sweetheart?" I ask, and she replies with a gasp.

"So close."

Slipping a finger into her sex, I suck on her clit, mimicking the motion of my hand until she is calling out my name.

"Jackson," she softly cries into the bedroom, a breeze whipping through the curtain brushing against our bodies.

Beneath me her languid body relaxes and sinks into the mattress. She looks up to me with a look on her face, a look I can't quite distinguish, but it sends a spark of fear through me. I thought I was prepared for this, for some sort of relationship. But fear claws at me. I'm not cut out for a pre-made family, am I? I'd screw it up. I'd screw her up more than she already is. I'd screw up those kids' lives. God, how can she even trust me around them?

I vault off the bed as if it's electrified me.

"I can't do a relationship."

She looks at me confused as if she hadn't considered the thought, which actually angers me more.

"Okay. . . I never asked."

My hand runs through my hair as I take in her perfect body lying on the bed.

"This can only be sex, Elle."

"Okay," she agrees again, and I nod before heading back to the window.

"You can use the door you know," she jokes as she watches me keenly, one arched brow cocked upward.

Instead, I hop through the window and turn around to look back at her.

"Lock this up behind me. You don't want anyone else slipping in," I say a bit more harshly than I intended.

"I can take care of myself, Jackson," she replies in the same tone.

"I want your lips on my cock next time," I add, just to see how much more I can rile her up. It's my new favorite game.

"You assume there will be a next time."

"Oh, there most definitely will be. Your pussy loves me."

"Why do you have to be so vile?" she asks shocked.

"You don't like the word pussy?"

"Only when it refers to a cat," she adds as she moves out of bed and leans out the window toward me.

I move closer, our faces only a few inches apart.

"I think you like it when I whisper it in your ear as I'm fucking you with my fingers."

"You'll never know," she says coyly, her eyes narrowing toward me.

My hand moves to her jaw and I cup her cheek in my palm, loving the way her soft skin feels in my hand. She closes her eyes, her body leaning toward me reflexively. My lips meet hers in a gentle kiss, a goodnight, a goodbye.

"Goodnight, Elle."

"Night, Jackson," she replies as I step away from her window and head across the yard.

Maybe her tearing down that fence is the best thing that could have happened, but I sure as hell won't be telling her that anytime soon.

Chapter Seven

Elle

MY PARENTS MADE THE four-hour drive to our home today to celebrate Kennedy's fourth birthday. They're all outside, Noah showing Nana and Pop-pop their new playset. And apparently they're all on the hunt for pirates. My dad offers to watch out for the small bounce house that I'm having delivered for a few of Kennedy's friends from her weekly playgroup.

The kids are great, the moms? Not so much. I haven't heard from Dan, but I'm hopeful that he and Sky, though it pains me, will attend the party. Today is

Kennedy's actual birthday and all she's asked for is a unicorn and her Daddy. It breaks my heart when I have to tell her that he lives in a different place now. She and Noah get to visit him once a month, but Sky refuses to let them visit at their old house. So far they've been to the library for reading time and that lasted about an hour.

I finish placing the pointed sugar cone on top of the cake shaped like a unicorn and take a step back. I'm pretty impressed with my creation if I do say so myself.

I smell him before I see him as Jackson steps through my open backdoor into the kitchen. After our night together last weekend I could spot his scent in a room of perfume. A bit manly, a bit woodsy, with a hint of fig. It's weird, but that's what I sense, and I want to bottle it up. I should probably sneak into his house and figure out what kind of soap he uses so I can keep some in my home.

After he snuck away from my bedroom the other night, I laid awake for hours. It's actually when I concocted the idea for the cake. But it wasn't just that. I was drunk on his kisses and high from his touch. My body tingled until the early hours of the morning when I finally caught an hour or two of shut-eye.

"Hey," he says from behind, his strong body sidling up against me. I didn't expect his touch so soon, since we had kind of ended things oddly last week and we haven't seen each other since.

"Hey, what do you think?" I ask, wanting his opinion on the unicorn head cake covered in white buttercream with a mane of pink and purple.

"You made that?" he asks in amazement as he steps around me and skirts around the island taking in all of its glory.

"I did. It came to me after you left last weekend."

"So I was a form of inspiration for this masterpiece," he states matter-of-factly. "I believe I deserve some sort of reward."

I watch the smirk grow on his face as he takes in my appearance from my toes to the top of my head.

"Aren't you already getting payment in the form of kisses?"

"Yeah, but I'm sure we could renegotiate new terms." He takes a step closer to me, bridging the already narrow gap between us.

"What kind of terms?" I inquire as his hand snakes around my waist as the other boxes me in against the counter.

"The kind where I find myself sneaking into your room as often as I'd like."

"I think that could be negotiable." I boldly lean into him, pressing our bodies together, our lips only a breath apart.

The patter of tiny feet makes themselves known as they pounce onto the deck quickly followed by my parents.

I step away from Jackson just as Noah and Kennedy slide into the house.

"Mommy, Mommy! The bouncy house is here!" Noah cries out enthusiastically while Kennedy's stare is riveted on the unicorn cake.

"Is that for me?" she whispers in astonishment.

Bending my knees, I squat down to her level. "It is. Do you like it?"

"It's beautiful!" she exclaims, her thin arms wrapping around my neck, burying her face into my shoulder.

"Only the best for my princess." Pulling back, I stand up and motion toward two cups of water I set aside for the kids and ask them to take a few sips before going back outside to play. I also remind them not to mess with the men putting up the bouncy house.

They scurry back outside to my parents and I turn back around to find Jackson squirting some of the remaining icing from the dispenser into his mouth. I admonish him with my gaze, you know – the "Mom look" – and he merely shrugs his shoulders and squirts a little more.

"Seems a shame for it to go to waste."

Laughing, I grab a few of the individual cupcakes I had baked and shove one in his direction.

"Instead of eating it, why don't you make yourself useful?"

His eyes widen in terror as if I've asked him to perform brain surgery.

"It doesn't have to look nice, Jackson. I'm covering them in sprinkles and glitter."

His stare of horror doesn't waiver.

"Please?" I whisper as I daringly press a small kiss to the corner of his chin.

"Fine," he huffs.

"Here," I begin as I place a cupcake in front of me and the pink frosting dispenser in my hand, "watch what I do."

I've already loaded the tips for the icing, so I simply swirl the frosting around the cupcake. Easy peasy. Jackson begins to decorate his cupcake, slowly rotating the dispenser around the top to mimic my design.

"Hey, I did it!" he announces joyfully, and I can't say that I'm surprised that his cupcake looks like a mirror image of my own.

"That looks great. You may have a calling as my assistant if you are ever looking for another job."

"I'll keep that in mind. Do you want me to help with the others?" he asks excitedly, and I bring over the pan containing ten more cupcakes.

It doesn't take long before we're done and covered in edible glitter and icing remnants. I'm standing at the sink trying to wash it off my hands and arms when I feel a pair of soft lips press against my bare shoulder.

"Jackson," I whisper as I peek out the window above the sink looking for the location of my parents. That's all I would need today is for them to walk in on Jackson and me. I'd never hear the end of the pestering.

"Sorry, you have some glitter here," he says, and then he presses another kiss to the side of my exposed neck. "And here."

"You know," I exhale as I close my eyes and lean against him, the water still pouring from the faucet. "For someone that doesn't like me, you sure can't seem to keep your lips to yourself."

He's now at the skin right below my ear, a space that I didn't realize could send a spark straight to my lady-bits if kissed the way Jackson is doing now. A lick, a nip, a kiss. A constant rotation of pain and pleasure.

"My lips have a mind of their own. No use controlling them," he replies, and I vaguely notice that he doesn't respond to still disliking me.

"What else can your lips do?"

At my question his hands slip under my shirt and reach upward, cupping my breasts through my plain cotton bra. Now I wish I had put something more feminine on this morning, but Jackson doesn't seem to mind as he tugs the cups down and exposes my breasts.

"I think you know what my lips can do," he replies, and then he slides my nipples between his two fingers as a deep growl sounds from his chest instantly, exciting my body. "Fuck. Turn around."

Jackson doesn't wait for me to move. Instead, he spins my body with his own hands, bringing my body against his. Before I even have a chance to realize what is taking place, one of his strong hands slides around the back of my thigh and slips underneath my cutoff jean shorts and panties bringing his fingers to my slick center. His other hand cups the back of my neck and brings our mouths together in a fevered kiss.

His fingers thrust in and out of my core. He's not gentle, instead he's pushing at a punishing pace, and if I weren't so wet and needy for him, it would be painful. Instead,it's not nearly enough. I want more. More of his touch, more of his kisses, just more of Jackson.

"You're so wet, Elle," he whispers against my lips.

"I'm so close," I cry out as I rock my hips against his hand seeking my release.

I throw my head back as I get closer to my pinnacle and I know I just barely escaped from banging my head on the upper cabinets.

"Yes," I whisper when I'm within reach, and then I hear a cry out the window and all movement stops.

Orgasm long forgotten, I rush out of Jackson's hold without a backward glance and make my way through the yard to find Noah on the ground holding his knee.

It takes a few minutes to clean him up and learn that he was trying to jump out of the swing but missed his landing. When I return to the house, I notice that Jackson is long gone. Somehow I missed him leaving. Which means I need to finish decorating and get myself ready with my body aching to finish what he started. Usually, I'd take care of it myself but I just won't have the time today.

I decide to go ahead and change my clothes for the party. I've set out a pretty yellow sundress since the party will be outside. In my bedroom, I notice something on the dresser and I cautiously approach it before bursting out in laughter.

In the middle sits the dispenser of icing with a note saying that he wants to use it later.

Guess that means I'll be leaving the window open tonight.

The party is in full force as the handful of kids jump around the unicorn shaped bounce house. I didn't even know that they made such a thing, but once I saw it on the website, I knew that Kennedy would have to have it. No other bounce house will do. Luckily, I promised the owner I would bake his daughter's birthday cake, so he gave me a steep discount on the rental.

We've already opened the presents and eaten as much cake as their little tummies can handle and now they're burning off that excess energy. I pour a few cups of lemonade, pink per Kennedy's request, and set out the cups for the kids and parents to grab. I'm secretly hoping that the parents will begin corralling their children back home, but that doesn't seem to be the case.

As I look around the yard, my already hot temper fires up more. My parents are relaxing on the deck with Dan's parents and Jackson's, who so kindly accepted the invitation last weekend. They were both smitten with the children and adding two more people didn't break the bank with the food order I had placed.

That also means Jackson is attending the party, and as I suspected, all of the mothers are huddled around him. He's only one of two men our age in attendance, and it seems like the mothers are frantically seeking his attention. I even witnessed the other single mother slipping her number in his back pocket earlier.

He's not mine. I completely understand that part, but it hurts all the same. My crazy mind feels like he's cheating and I'm having a hard time telling myself that he's not.

And to top it all off, Dan hasn't shown up. He is missing his daughter's fourth birthday, and if he thinks she hasn't noticed, he would be dead wrong. Right after she blew out her candles she asked where her daddy was. She had wished to have a family again, and it took all my strength to not simultaneously cry on the spot and go find Dan to beat some sense into him.

All the parents had looked at me in pity and that may have been the worst part of all. That look in their eyes that I have been trying to avoid for months. The look that I couldn't keep my husband and that I'm the reason my daughter's wish won't come true.

"Hey," Scott, the single father in attendance says, startling me, causing some of the lemonade to spill from the pitcher. Luckily I'm using disposable tablecloths.

"Hey, Scott. Are you and Toby having a good time?" I ask as I smooth down my dress, which causes Scott's attention to fall to my legs. It's then that I notice how short my dress really is, exposing the majority of my thighs.

"Um. . .the party is great. You've kind of ruined any of us for birthday parties at this point. Yours have always been the best, but this is - wow."

"Thanks," I reply, blushing slightly at the praise.

I watch Scott as he fiddles with his watch, turns to check on Toby in the bounce house, and then brings his gaze back to me. Scott is handsome, no one can argue that, with his dark hair, yearly tan, and black framed glasses. He's probably feeling the loss from Jackson's attention since the mothers in our playgroup usually flock to him relentlessly.

"So, I wanted to see how you were doing. Are you and the kids adjusting well?"

Scott lost his wife in a car accident right after Toby was born.

"I think we're doing the best we can. Of course, it would help if their father was more involved," I disclose, instantly wishing that I could take it back. I don't need to be sharing my burdens.

"Well, if you ever want to get together and take the kids somewhere let me know. Toby would love it." I watch in fascination as he reaches into his back pocket and pulls out a business card.

"Are you. . .are you asking me on a date?" I ask confused.

"Maybe? I think so. I haven't done this in a long time," he explains shyly, a smattering of red creeping up his face.

I'm kind of surprised that the first time he asks out someone, it just happens to be me. And then I wonder if he's been crushing on me since I joined the playgroup when Kennedy was a baby.

"I don't know. I haven't really thought about dating, to be honest. I've had a lot going on. But when I decide that I'm ready I'll give you a call, okay?"

He nods his head, and I can tell that the rejection stings but I'm being honest, I'm not ready to date. At least I don't think I am. That's why my arrangement with Jackson works so well.

As if my thought of him can conjure his attention, I watch from the corner of my eye as Jackson pulls away from his harem of mothers and makes his way to where I stand.

Scott's gaze notices his approach as well and his shoulders sink down slightly, and I do begin to feel a bit bad for him. He grabs a lemonade from the table and heads toward the vacated group without a backward glance.

"What did you and mister CFO discuss?"

"CFO?" I reply as Jackson moves behind the table to stand next to me. His business card does seem thick and important. I hadn't paid close attention to the embossed words.

"Yep, he and I were chatting earlier about business things. Very boring."

"It can't be as boring as this party is to you. You don't even have kids."

"Elle," he says, pulling my attention away from pouring more glasses of lemonade. He waits until I'm looking at him in the eye to continue. "We both know that I'm not here for the party."

Somehow all the air escapes my lungs and I struggle to ask, "What are you here for?"

One of his fingers tugs on a curl hanging over my shoulder. "I'm here for the cake, of course. Always the cake."

"You're an asshole," I reply, and his laughter draws everyone's attention.

Great. I'm standing here red from embarrassment and with wet panties because being within a five-foot radius of Jackson has my body melting on the spot. Let's not even mention that I've been on the verge of an orgasm since I had to pull away this morning.

"Yeah, I know," he replies smugly as if I've complimented him. "My parents are raving about the cake, by the way. They may ask you to cater their anniversary party."

"Oh, that would be fun. I'd be happy to. Just tell them to give me a date before they leave."

A small stack of cups suddenly falls to the ground at our feet and Jackson bends down to grab them, telling me to stay where I am. At first, I'm confused by his demand, but as he begins to stand he reaches out and trails the back of my leg with the tips of his fingers.

"Jackson. . .I-"

"Don't move, Elle. No one can see anything," he insists as he stands to his full height placing the stack of cups back on the table, his other hand slowly moving across my panties before moving the fabric to the side to expose my center. "Pretend like you're doing something and I'll continue. If you stop, I stop."

"What do you want me to do?" I ask as I spy my cupcake container nearby. I can start to pack them up.

"Don't care," he responds as his thumb brushes against my clit and I have to grip the edge of the table hard.

"Are you sure no one can see?"

"I'm sure. No one is paying us any attention."

My shaking hand reaches out to grasp one of the cupcakes and gently places it into the container as Jackson begins to slide one of his fingers deep inside my sex. Somehow he's able to find my most sensitive spot and I almost drop the cupcake as my legs practically give out.

"So sensitive," he whispers. "I bet you're still waiting to come, aren't you? You didn't even get yourself off after you left the kitchen this morning. Your muscles are pulling my finger so hard."

"I couldn't," I breathlessly reply as I place another cupcake in the container, my eyes darting around the yard where no one pays us any mind.

"Do you want to come now?" Jackson asks, as his free arm wraps around my waist and tugs my body against him. His grip on my abdomen is hard and firm, as if he's using my body to control his own needs.

"Yes, please," I plead as I feel my orgasm forming in my body, the waves of pleasure building with every pass of his finger in my core.

Then a new sensation occurs and I'm lost in the feeling. His thumb caresses the rim of my most secret place, a place untouched, and it catapults me over the edge. I bite my lip so hard to keep from crying out that I can taste a trickle of blood on my tongue.

That is the most intense orgasm I've ever had, and now I will be spending the remainder of the party wishing for another.

As I begin to come back into myself, I realize that Jackson has taken a significant step away from me. I turn to look at him, thank him, but I can't decipher the grimace on his face. Is it regret?

"Jackson, I. . .," I begin, but my mother steps up to the table.

"Hi, sweetie. Your dad and I are going to head back. It was a wonderful party."

I skirt around the table and wrap my arms around my mother. We haven't always had the best relationship since the divorce, but she and my father finally spoke the other night and I can see that they're trying to make an effort.

"Thank you for making the trip. I know Kennedy and Noah loved having you here."

"We wouldn't have missed it. It was nice to see Dan's parents too. It's been a while. Oh, Jackson," my mother says as she looks over my shoulder. "It was wonderful to meet you and your parents today. Keep an eye on my little girl, okay?"

"Yes, ma'am," Jackson replies, but I don't miss the glimmer sparkling in his eye. Yeah, he'll make sure to keep a special eye on me.

"Love you, Elle. And let us know how the contract meeting goes," my mother mentions in passing. She must have been speaking with Sara.

"I will. Love you too."

I wave them off with Jackson by my side, which feels a bit weird and right at the same time, but I don't have a chance to think about it further when Dan's parents say their goodbyes, and finally the rest of the party-goers make their way to their cars.

The crew comes to pick up the bounce house and then I gaze out at the mess in my yard from my kitchen. Who knew four-year-olds could destroy so much grass? I hadn't anticipated so much cleanup after the party, but as I watch Kennedy and Noah in the living room opening all of her new toys, I know that now is a better time than any to do it and get it over with.

I'm surprised to find Jackson and his dad tossing away plates and cups left behind while his mother repackages some of the food.

Rushing out into the yard I exclaim, "You guys don't have to do this."

Jackson's mother, Naomi, stares at me as she fastens the cupcake container and I instantly blush as I remember what Jackson did to me earlier. "Sometimes it's okay to ask for help. You'd be here for hours if you did this by yourself. And it's not like we're going far."

By the tone in her voice, I know better than to argue. She has the "mom voice" down pat. I should try to learn from her.

"Yes, ma'am. I appreciate the help."

I help Naomi finish packing up the food and desserts while Stan begins folding the tables I rented.

"What else can I do?" Jackson asks as he helps me carry a few of the platters inside to store in the fridge.

"I think all that's left is to attempt to pick up any of the confetti and streamers in the yard and look for any leftover candy from the piñata. I don't want any of it to end up in your yard or my kids' mouths."

Jackson laughs deep in his chest as we step back outside. "You know, this is the perfect time to mention that a fence would help with that."

I gaze at him in mock anger, my eyes narrowing just the slightest bit. "You shush it."

"Just stating a fact," he says, bending over to pick up a few pieces of candy and paper confetti.

"Yeah, yeah."

The four of us work together for another fifteen minutes, and finally my yard begins to resemble what it had been before the party began.

"Whew, who knew four-year-olds could be so destructive?" Stan asks as he takes a seat in one of the patio chairs.

"I know, right? I was asking myself the same thing. Thank you all for your help. Can I get you a drink or anything? I have a few beers in the fridge."

"I think we're okay," Stan replies. "I don't remember kids being so exhausting. I think we're going to go take a nap." He laughs, and Naomi eagerly nods her head in agreement.

"I hear ya. I wish I could take a nap, but I'm pretty sure Noah and Kennedy will be wired for hours. We're going out for pizza tonight if you all want to come. The kids would be thrilled."

"They aren't going with their dad?" Jackson asks from behind, startling me.

"That is a subject I really don't want to discuss, but please," I say, turning my attention back to Jackson's parents, "we'd love to have you join us. We were going around six."

Naomi looks up at Jackson who is standing behind me and then her already radiant smile grows.

"Sounds like fun, we'll be there."

I'm not sure what passed between her and her son, but either he nodded and said they could go or he shook his head furiously and that egged her on. With Jackson, it's hard to say.

"Alright, we'll see you tonight. Just text Jackson when you're leaving," Naomi insists as she stands, Stan quickly following.

"Oh, I don't have Jackson's number."

"Oh, dear," Naomi says as if I've told her something truly shocking. Because why would I ask for the number of the man that's only been nice to me three times in the month that I've known him? "Jackson, sweetie, give her your number. What if there was an emergency?"

I guess she does have a point.

"I don't have my phone on me. It's inside."

Jackson comes closer with his phone in his hand and asks me for my number. After I give it to him, he sends a text from his phone to mine.

"Thanks," I whisper as I look up at him, his blue eyes matching the color of the clear summer sky.

"So, I'll see you later?" he asks after his parents leave the deck and begin walking back to his house.

"Sure. I mean, the kids would love to have you come to dinner. It's just pizza, not a date or anything," I scramble as I try to make sure he realizes that I know we're only doing the casual thing.

"I know, Elle."

He peers over his shoulder and before I have a chance to say anything more he bends down and presses his lips against mine. This isn't just any kiss like before, he is devouring me as if I'm his first taste of sugar. Before I know it he's pulling back and stepping off the deck.

"I've been wanting to do that all day. I'll see you tonight."

Breathless I reply, "Okay," before I'm watching his backside as he retreats across the yard.

I take a moment to gather myself then I turn inside to find Kennedy and Noah playing with some of the toys she received today. Apparently, we're playing dragons versus unicorns. They're so lost in their battle that they don't even hear me step inside and tell them that our new friends are joining us for dinner.

My phone pings on the kitchen counter and I remember that I need to program Jackson's number into the contact list. I unlock the screen and see the first of two messages.

Unknown Number: This is Jackson.

With a smirk on my lips, I program his number into my phone with the first thing that comes to mind then read his second message.

> **AHole Neighbor: You look sexy as hell in that dress. I can still feel you coming on my fingers.**

My muscles contract in another small wave just remembering how he made me come apart with just his hand, something no one else has been able to do. I've always had to make myself come with a vibrator.

For a second I consider changing his contact name, but then another message comes across.

> **AHole Neighbor: I found a shoe in my yard. Why the fuck would someone leave a party with their kid missing a shoe? This is why there was a fence.**

Then I remember that he really is a certified asshole despite his occasional niceties.

After getting the kids cleaned up and changed, because grass stains don't always look so nice when you're at dinner, I barely have enough time to change and recharge myself.

In a rush, I throw on a blue wrap dress that I've had hanging in my closet forever. Dan always hated that it showed off a hint of cleavage, so I've never worn it. Today seems like the perfect opportunity. Most of the curls I put in my hair this morning have fallen, so I pull a brush through my hair and leave just the ends with a hint of a curl remaining. I refresh my makeup with a few swipes of eyeshadow and one recoating of mascara before the alarm sounds on my phone signaling that it's time to leave.

I shoot a text to Jackson, and as I wrangle the kids out the door, he's standing beside my SUV waiting for us. I almost stumble down the steps as I take him in. His dark jeans hang low on his hips and they wrap around his muscular thighs. I bet from behind, the denim cups his ass perfectly. He's wearing a faded red V-neck shirt that molds to his body like a second skin. The shape of his chest and abs are clearly defined beneath the soft material.

His arms flex as I make my way toward him and I'm surprised that the sleeves of the shirt don't break at the seams. The kids jump around him, excited for him to be joining them tonight, but his focus lies solely on me, searing my skin with his penetrating gaze.

"Hey," I call out as I step off the walkway onto the gravel about a foot away from him.

Since Jackson doesn't respond immediately, I open the back door to let Kennedy inside the car, while Noah is already inside and strapped in after opening the door on the other side. I finish buckling all of Kennedy's straps and then close the door to find Jackson still leaning against the car in the same manner, his eyes never leaving me.

I notice his parents' in their car idling on the street and ask, "Are you not riding with your parents?"

"I'm thirty-two-years-old. I'm pretty sure it would embarrass my parents as much as it would me, to ride with them."

"You're probably right," I reply as he opens the driver's side door. "Thanks. I didn't know you knew how to be a gentleman."

"I'm full of surprises." Just as he is about to close the door Jackson leans in, whispering in my ear, "You look beautiful in this dress, by the way. I can't wait to unwrap it and see it on the floor."

"Oh, glad you. . .um. . .approve," I stutter, surprised by the way my heart pounds at his words.

Jackson doesn't say anything more. He skirts around the car and slips into the passenger side, then I put the car in drive and head toward Kennedy's favorite restaurant.

Halfway through the trip, Jackson takes hold of the hand I have loosely resting on my thigh and twines our fingers together. I try to keep my eyes on the road but the gesture is so unlike him that I find myself glancing down at our hands every so often.

"You surprise me," I say as the red, white, and green sign for the pizza place comes into view. I pull my hand away, missing the warmth of his grasp.

"I surprise myself, Elle," Jackson replies as he looks out the window, but I don't miss the way his eyebrows furrow in confusion. He seems as baffled as I am at which Jackson I'm going to get. Either the asshole or the gentleman.

Trying to change the subject I ask, "Have you been here before?" I realize that it's on the other side of town, but I don't know much about Jackson and where he grew up.

"I haven't, no."

"Well, they have a bit of everything if you don't want pizza. But it's the best."

"I'll take your word for it."

He probably doesn't even eat pizza since he's a personal trainer. I hadn't even considered that when I asked him to join us. Jackson makes a move to exit the car but I grip his forearm with my hand, holding him back.

"I didn't think to ask if you can eat Italian food. I can take you somewhere else. Somewhere healthier."

"It's fine, Elle. I can eat whatever I want."

"I'm sorry, it's just that I should have asked earlier."

"If I couldn't eat anything or didn't want to come I wouldn't be here. It's fine. Plus, it's for Kennedy's birthday," he says as he peers over the back of the seat at Kennedy playing with a Barbie in her carseat. This is the Jackson I like to be around, the sweet and considerate one. "Now, stay there. I'll come get you," he commands. There is the asshole, I mentally remind myself and laugh as he opens the door.

"Something amusing you?"

"No, not at all."

If only he knew the thoughts in my head.

Chapter Eight

Jackson

T HE PIZZA PLACE IS bustling when we enter and I watch in horror as kids rush back and forth in the restaurant, their parents paying them little mind. My head begins to ache at the screaming, reminding me of my pact to remain relationship free, but as I look down at the birthday girl holding my hand, it all ceases to exist. Kennedy looks around the space and her eyes widen when she watches all the kids run about. I notice that her hand tightens in mine and she takes a step closer to me. Noah does the same with his mom as she puts her name down for a table with the young hostess.

"It seems there is a birthday party going on. It's going to be a few minutes before we're seated," Elle explains as she steps back toward my parents and me.

My parents take a seat on the bench close to the door and we move to follow, but as I take a step a kid comes out of nowhere and practically plows into Kennedy. Out of instinct, or fear, I haul the little girl up into my arms and hold her close. She immediately rests her head on my shoulder and something inside me shifts. I don't know if my heart is growing three or four times its size like the green guy's heart in that Christmas cartoon, or if my need to protect people is coming out in full force, but that constant emptiness I've always felt in my chest dissipates. That emptiness that always made me feel that I couldn't love someone, which is why I broke things off with my girlfriend from high school. I didn't believe I could do something serious, that I didn't have it in me. Maybe I had it all along and it took the instant love of a little girl to set the spark.

"Shit," I whisper to myself but Kennedy must hear because she whispers back, "Mommy says that's a bad word."

I turn my gaze to look at Elle standing beside the bench where Noah has secured a spot on my Dad's lap. She looks stunning tonight in that blue dress. It's simple and classic just like her. I can't believe she wasted all those years with her ex or that he had the nerve to cheat on her. Elle is one of the most beautiful women I've ever seen in my life. She's beautiful without even trying and she doesn't even know it.

She must sense my gaze on her because she looks up from her cell phone she had been typing on and locks her gaze on me. I can see in her eyes that watching me hold her daughter is doing something to her. At first I think she's upset, but her lips part to reveal a beautiful smile. The kind of smile someone has when they've won a gold medal or bought their first house or married their soul mate. That kind of smile. And I secretly hope that I'm part of the reason behind it.

"Table for Knight?" the hostess calls out, and the spell is broken instantly.

We follow her to a table in the corner, far away from the rest of the screaming kids, thank God. It doesn't take long for us to order and receive our food. My parents claim that it's the best pizza they've ever had, but I don't taste any of it. My focus is on Elle and the way she savors each bite of her food. Her eyes closing as she relishes in the flavors, her pink tongue reaching out to taste a morsel on her lips. It's mesmerizing.

My mom must catch me staring at Elle across the way because she kicks me with her foot under the table before laughing to herself.

"Funny, Mom."

"I like her, and her kids are so well behaved."

She's right, both Noah and Kennedy sit quietly eating their pizza and coloring a sheet of paper beside Elle.

Soon everyone is done eating and we say goodbye to my parents, Elle considering their offer of watching the kids sometime. I can tell she's wary of strangers being around her family, but my parents are already in love with Noah and Kennedy. They are the grandchildren they've always wanted.

Back at the house the kids still seem wired from today. I would have thought they would be ready to crash but apparently for kids, sugar doesn't work that way.

"Mister Jackson, can you stay and watch a movie with us?" Noah asks me then turns his attention to his mom requesting the same.

"Noah, it's late, and I'm sure Jackson has had enough time with kids today. Plus you both need to take a bath."

Time with Elle in the dark? Where can I sign up?

"What movie are you thinking, Noah?" I interrupt, and I can see that Elle wants to stomp her foot in protest.

"*How to Train Your Dragon?*" he asks, hoping I'll say yes to his version of a cool guy movie.

"Dragons?"

"Yes!" he exclaims as he jumps out of the car once we're in the driveway. "So many dragons. It's my favorite. Do you like dragons?"

"What's not to like about dragons?" I reply, but my question is directed to Elle.

"Please, Mom. I'll wash up really good, and we can have popcorn."

Apparently popcorn is the way to Elle's heart since I watch the smile blossom on her lips.

"Noah, I'm only going to allow this because you start kindergarten in another week and it's still Kennedy's birthday. Or it was," she whispers as she pulls a sleeping Kennedy from her carseat.

The little boy grumbles as he watches his mom carry his sleeping sister inside their house and I kneel down beside him.

"You still want to watch the movie, little man?"

He nods his head and looks at me with sad eyes.

"Well, why don't you go inside, wash yourself, and get ready for bed without asking your mom for help? Then maybe she'll consider letting you stay up for the movie."

"Okay, Mister Jackson."

I watch as he scurries off, eager to show how grown up he is and I casually walk into Elle's house. I haven't seen the living room for more than a minute and

I'm surprised at how lived in it looks. She's hung pictures on the walls and around the television hangs a few items that look like they came from a barn.

Is that part of a windmill? Where can you even buy that shit?

But the strange thing is that it all works, and I like it. It definitely suits her style. On the fireplace mantle sits a heap of pictures. Some of the kids as babies, some of Elle with the kids, some of Elle with the blonde from the other day. Then I focus in on the family picture in the far corner. Elle stands with her hand on each of the kid's shoulders, Noah and Kennedy a couple of years younger than they are now, and there is a man beside her with his arm wrapped around her gripping her shoulder tightly. You can almost see the grimace on her face beneath that smile. So this is Dan, the man that cheated on his wife with her best friend and knocked her up.

I'm not sure how long I'm standing in front of the picture but Noah comes bounding into the room wearing a pair of Star Wars pajamas.

"Oh," Elle says as she walks into the room carrying what looks like a DVD in her hand. "I wasn't sure if you were serious about staying."

"Of course I'm staying. There are dragons involved," I reply and I watch in fascination as Noah cracks up laughing, practically falling off his seat on the couch.

Elle gets the DVD set up and I take the seat next to Noah.

We don't even get to the point where Noah requests the popcorn because after ten minutes into the movie he passes out against me, his tiny body molded against my side.

"Well, that didn't last long," I whisper to Elle, breaking her focus on the movie.

She turns her gaze to me and then looks at Noah, a soft smile on her lips.

"I didn't think it would. He wants to be a big kid so bad and I just want him to stay little forever."

I run my hand through Noah's soft brown hair and wonder what it felt like when he was born. Was it just as soft or has it changed as he has grown?

"They all grow up sometime. Do you want me to carry him to bed?"

"That's okay. I like to carry him while he'll still let me." She smiles as she stands and bends down to lift Noah against her body, his body morphing around hers.

I follow behind her as she carries him into his room and stand in the doorway as she tucks him in. It feels surreal to be here watching this moment between them but I'm powerless to turn away.

"You have really good kids," I say to her as she steps out of the room and closes the door.

"Thanks." She gazes up at me and bites her lip nervously. "Do you. . .do you want to stay?"

I can see how much bravery it took her to ask the question, her fear of rejection palpable around her. Instead of giving her a response I lean forward and kiss her. The spark of attraction between us is just as powerful today as it was that first moment she called me an asshole.

Her arms wrap around my neck as she presses her body against me. Reaching out, I grip her thighs with my hands and lift her up, forcing her to wrap those gorgeous legs around my waist. I can feel her hot core as she rests against my waist, the heat seeping through my shirt to my skin. I moan as I imagine how it will feel against my cock.

We move toward the other end of the hall where I know her bedroom is located, but before we get there some primal instinct inside of me takes over. In the hallway just outside her door, I slam her body against the wall and pull away from her mouth with our hips still joined.

"Fuck, you're gorgeous," I tell her as I take in her mussed hair and puffy pink lips.

Her hands are braced against the wall as I rock against her body once, eliciting that beautiful moan I want to hear from her lips. I kiss her again, the need to taste her overpowering me. Her fingers pause at the edge of my shirt, her uncertainty reminding me that she's not as experienced as my past lovers.

"Touch me, Elle," I whisper against her mouth, my restraint about to snap like a rubber band.

Her eyes widen as she gazes at me, our stare penetrating the last of her fear. I can tell when she gives in to her desire because that tongue I've become addicted to peeks out between her lips just as her fingers reach inside my shirt caressing the soft skin at my back. My grip tightens around her thighs, my control slowly slipping, then I'm pulling her away from the wall and I can hear myself murmuring something about a bed.

Somehow I make it into the bedroom with her lips pressed against my neck. Her bed is neatly made, and normally I would feel bad for tossing her on top of the fresh linens, but my need for her is overpowering.

I fling her in the middle of the bed, her body bouncing a few times before it settles. Reaching behind my head, I tug my shirt over my body and throw it aimlessly into the room. Her gasp of air doesn't go unnoticed and I smirk as she realizes that I've heard it. I toe off my shoes and socks before placing a knee on the bed and then the other, crawling over her perfect body still covered by her dress.

I press a kiss to one of her bent knees and continue my path until I'm kneeling between her legs.

"You're wearing too many clothes," I say as I tug on the bow resting at her waist.

The dress falls open in front of me and it's like Christmas day. Her glowing white skin glistens in the moonlight shining through the window. I lean over her and inspect the black lace that covers her breasts and the pair of matching panties that do the same with her mound. Her soft breasts heave behind their entrapment and I long to free them, but my attention is quickly replaced as I feel the soft touch of her fingers on my arm. My hold almost releases at her gentleness.

I can feel the groan building in my chest as her fingers move up my bicep and across my shoulder before trailing down to my chest.

"I never imagined your skin would be so soft. Everything about you is so hard," she whispers, and she's right. I am hard. My cock is pulsating beneath my jeans begging for its escape.

Bending my elbows, I frame her face with my arms and lean down to kiss her sweet lips. I'm so addicted to her taste I could kiss her for eternity. Elle's fingers slide up and down my back as she responds to my kiss, her body becoming more pliant beneath me. Releasing one of my arms, I slide it between our bodies until I come in contact with her already wet panties. I love that I don't even have to touch her for her to be wet and ready for me.

I stroke her a few times on the outside, her body shivering with each pass, then I slip underneath the material and feel the instant heat of her body's response to me.

"Jackson," she whispers against my lips as I stroke my fingers through her slick folds.

She shyly reaches for the button on my jeans, her fingers fumbling as she tries to release the button. My straining cock is already peeking out over the top of my jeans and it jerks every time her hand passes across the tip. I had gone commando this evening, not because I knew that Elle and I would get to this point, but because I had been hopeful.

Once she has the button unfastened and the zipper down, my erection falls forward seeking out Elle's sex. Her eyes widen at the size, probably because I'm much larger than her asshole ex, but I can only assume. I am bigger than most guys.

The surprise in her eyes diminishes quickly as she tentatively wraps her hand around the base of my shaft. Her soft palm against the sensitive skin triggers a growl from deep in my chest.

Her movements start off slow and erratic. Removing my hand from between her legs, which causes a moan of disapproval from her, I wrap my hand around hers and show her how I like to be stroked – base to tip with her thumb or palm stroking across the head and coating my erection in the pre-cum.

I stroke along with her three times and thank fuck she is a quick learner because she eagerly continues the movements on her own while I go back to touching her sex. I slide my fingers through her heat, coating myself in her warmth, and then I slide two fingers inside her before removing them quickly and repeating the motion. It takes her a second, just a moment, to focus on her own pleasure before she realizes that I'm mimicking her strokes on my cock as I thrust my fingers in her body.

Something about this notion must encourage her because her caresses begin to quicken, the pace almost enough to have me blowing my load too soon.

"Elle," I groan as I drop my forehead against hers. "That feels too good, sweetheart. I'm going to come if you don't stop."

"Don't you want to come?" she asks, but her focus is still between our bodies as her hand slowly slides up and down my angry cock.

"I do, but not like this. I want to be inside you."

"Sorry, the skin is so soft, like velvet or suede."

Internally, I pray that she stops soon or I won't be able to control my need to thrust between her legs. My first time with her I planned on being gentle, taking my time, but right now she's going to sever that piece of thread holding onto my sanity.

Luckily, as I press the heel of my hand against her clit all of her movements stop as her body trembles beneath me. Her release is quick, surprising both her and me as she grips the sheet beneath her and the base of my cock as she rides it out against my hand. I could stare at her for hours watching her fall over the cliff of pleasure. Her eyes flutter closed as she takes in every sensation and her lips form this perfect "O" before morphing into the tiniest of smiles. It's captivating. And I want to watch it happen again.

Before she is completely free from her release, I'm escaping the confines of my jeans. I make sure to reach for my wallet and snag the stack of condoms I stuffed inside this afternoon. I'm not sure we'll use all of them but I'd rather be prepared because I most certainly wouldn't mind spending the night between Elle's legs repeatedly.

Hovering over her once more, I slant my body over hers and reach behind her sated body to release the clasp of her bra. Expertly it snaps free after my first attempt and I pull the straps down Elle's arms just as her eyes flicker open.

"You're sexy as hell when you come, Elle," I tell her as I tilt my head forward and kiss a path from her shoulder down to the peak of her breast.

Using one of my arms I hold myself up as I taste her skin, circling her nipple with my tongue, and use my other hand to slide the nipple of her other breast between my fingers. Her hand, which had so expertly stroked my cock, now gently trails up and down my forearm. The movement is unhurried as she takes in the pleasure of me tasting her, but it sends waves of desire straight to my erection as if it is a direct wavelength.

"Can I make you come like this, sweet girl? Just with my mouth on your breast?"

I peek up at her as I switch my mouth to her other breast, giving it equal opportunity between my lips, and she nods just as her fingers tighten around my arm, her movements halting. She's close again, the precipice just out of her reach as she rocks her hips against my thigh. I bring it closer, giving her the source of friction she needs, and it's beyond erotic to feel her wetness coating my leg as she seeks her release.

"Jackson," she whispers as her small nails dig into my arm, the bit of pain welcome.

This time as she orgasms at my touch I take a moment to sit back onto my knees and slide one of the condoms on my shaft, the purple head pulsating beneath my touch as I slide the latex down.

I don't slide right home. Instead, I rest above her, waiting for Elle to give me the cue that she is ready. Her breathing begins to slow as she comes back to herself and I wait patiently for her to give me the go ahead. I'll leave if she's finished for the night but I am secretly praying to all that is holy that she'll let me inside her. I need to be inside her.

Using my fingers, I stroke against her slit waiting for her to respond, and luckily her response comes quickly.

"I want more, Jackson," she speaks softly as she licks her lips, her eyes taking me in beneath her hooded lids.

"I'll go slow, baby," I say, moving my body on top of hers, my cock nudging at her entrance. I know she is tight, ridiculously so after having two children, so I need to be slow with her, gentle.

I pull back after just the tip makes its way inside and then I'm repeating the motion again, a little bit more with every pass. By the time I make it halfway I can tell that Elle is feeling the fullness inside her, tiny waves passing over my cock as it slips inside her channel. Her lids are closed but I want to see her, all of her.

"Elle, look at me," I request as I gaze down, her eyes popping open immediately. "I want to see you. How does it feel?"

"Full. Tight."

"I'm almost there, sweetheart. I'm trying to go slow."

I ease out of her again before plunging inside about three-quarters of the way this time.

"I want all of it, Jackson. I want all of you."

I can hear her unspoken meaning, whether she intends for it or not. I know that she's not in the place yet to want more. Hell, I didn't even realize that I was until earlier, but I'll get her there. I'll show her that there is more than she knows, more than what she's been given in life. I can start with here, now, because it's obvious she's never experienced true pleasure. Never experienced true, animalistic passion.

With a final thrust, I plunge deep inside, her body fighting at first, Elle's features distorting at the intrusion, but then the walls of her sex relax and grip me firmly, Elle's face transforming into bliss.

I don't move my hips, I let her body adjust to me as I take both of her hands and hold them above her head. Leaning forward I kiss her slick lips, our tongues dueling as I wait for a sign that she's ready. Elle's hips move upward just a smidge, the tiniest hint that she wants more.

I pull out of her and slide back in, my shaft covered in her wetness, her sex tightening around me as if it never wants me to leave. And there is no other place I'd rather be. We continue to kiss as I thrust in and out of her body until I can no longer hold back my control.

I rear back, using one hand to keep her wrists in place and the other to rub small circles on her clit as I pound into her body. Elle responds by opening her legs wider than before, giving me more access to the sweetness between her legs.

"Fuck, you feel good. I'm gonna come, sweetheart. I need you to get there," I announce as my hips hammer into her, our slick skin slapping together in the quiet room.

"I'm there. Oh God," she cries out as her core tightens around me further than I thought was possible. "Jackson!" she shouts on a gasp as her body vibrates in waves around me, her fingers flex beneath my hold as she pushes her release completely from her body.

I want to memorize how she looks right now: head tossed back in pleasure, back arched, eyes closed, the tiniest of smiles on her lips; this is everything lovemaking should look like.

A few more thrusts into her quivering pussy and I feel myself release into the condom with the strangest of wishes that I had been able to come deep inside her. But that's a crazy notion, especially since I'm still trying to come to terms with the fact that I may actually want to try a relationship with her. My body jerks inside her bringing me back to the moment but I'm not ready to pull away. Instead, I find myself leaning forward once again and resting my forehead against Elle's, her satiated smile welcoming me closer to her.

"That was. . .amazing, Elle."

"I didn't know that it could be like that," she whispers, seemingly in a trance.

I comb my fingers through some of the loose hair around her face as I gaze into her eyes and try to gauge how she is feeling.

"And how is that?" I whisper as I press another kiss to her lips because I can't control myself. This girl is already changing the game for me. Usually, I'm out before the woman has even realized that I've left. Now I want nothing more than to bury myself so far into Elle that she feels me for weeks.

"Like it's more," she replies wearily. "And that scares me."

"Why is that scary?" I whisper against her mouth. I'm only half listening because my mind is focused on the fact that my cock is still firmly planted inside her.

"Because . . . I don't know if I can do this, especially with you. It's been a week and this is just supposed to be fun and casual. Jackson, this tonight didn't feel casual and I just got out of a bad marriage. You don't need my baggage and you said yourself that you aren't ready for a family."

"Elle," I say as I roll over onto my back, dislodging my cock and pulling her with me, her head resting on my chest. "Something changed today. I don't know what but I want something with you. Something

I've never wanted with anyone else, baggage and all. We'll go slow, alright? I'm in no rush."

She traces an indirect path on my chest, little squiggles made by her fingertips as she contemplates my suggestion. "I'm going to be bad at it. Look what happened last time."

"Well, I've only ever had one serious relationship, so we can both learn together, okay?"

She goes silent again, even her squiggles have stopped. Her breathing levels out and just when I think she's fallen asleep she turns her body so that she can rest her chin on my chest and look up at me.

"I have two conditions," she begins. "First, I want to think about it, okay? Maybe we can try and keep it to ourselves because I don't want to get the kids attached or anything if we mess it up."

"Sounds reasonable," I reply, stroking my hand through her mussed hair.

"And second, how many condoms did you bring? Because I would really like to do that again."

A wicked smile grows on her face and I find myself laughing as I take off the condom from earlier and toss it in the trashcan beside her nightstand.

"Don't you worry, sweetheart," I say as I tug on another condom, my cock already standing at full salute, and lie on my back. I move Elle's body so that she has to straddle my hips. "You're in control this time."

With a saucy grin on her lips, she rocks her hips against my cock, teasing me with everything she possesses before taking my cock in her hand and lining it up at her entrance, slowly sinking herself on my erection.

Watching her use me to reach her release is one of the most erotic things I've ever witnessed. The way her breasts bounce with each thrust, the way she tosses her head back when my cock slides against her most sensitive spot, the way her hands grip at my chest as she adjusts her position.

I growl as that tingling begins to build in my spine and with little finesse, I grip Elle's hips to steady her movements and begin to propel my cock deep within her.

"Oh my God," she cries out as our hips smack against each other until we're both toppling over the brink.

Our breaths come in heavy pants, both of us trying to come back into ourselves, and I'm waiting for Elle to tell me that she's had enough or that I'm too much for her. But that little minx surprises the hell out of me as she reaches across the bed and grabs a third condom, tossing it on my chest.

"Three?" she questions with a glint in her eye, and I'll be damned if I'm not growing hard again.

Scrambling off the bed, I toss the second condom in the wastebasket, then turn around to tug Elle by the legs to the edge of the bed.

"The question is, sweet girl, are you ready for round three?" I slide my hand in her wetness now coating her thighs and trail it to her backside, letting my thumb press against her tight pucker.

She groans in response before whispering my name like a plea, and I know that I have a long night ahead of me, but I'll be damned if I won't give this girl everything that she desires.

Now if only I can convince her to take a chance on us.

I wake early in the morning before the sun even begins to rise and it takes all my strength to leave the bed. I'm lying on my back with Elle wrapped in my arms, her petite body curved around me. Brushing some of the hair away from her face, I gaze down at the beauty that spent most of the night trying to wear me out. She wasn't successful. After about the fifth round she pretty much told me to get away from her. I would have laughed if she hadn't promptly passed out before I had even taken the last condom off my erection.

I tilt my head and brush my lips against her puckered mouth as if it's inviting me for a taste.

"I have to go open the gym, sweetheart."

She moans in response and cuddles closer to me. Damn if this isn't the first time I consider calling someone else to open.

"I'll see you later, okay?"

"Mmhmm," she replies as I press another kiss to her lips and scoot off the bed. I tug on my jeans lying at the foot of the bed, but in the darkness of the room, I'm not able to find my shirt. Oh well, I'll just grab it later.

I gently open her door and sneak out into the hall hoping not to wake anyone else in the house. I'm surprised to find Noah sitting at the kitchen counter in the dark, his face illuminated by the small light emitted by the microwave. He's got a bowl of cereal in front of him and the carton of milk still sitting out. At four in the morning, it is too early for a five-year-old to be awake.

"Hey, little man, what are you doing awake?" I ask as I approach him quietly in the kitchen. I'm not sure if he suffers from somnambulism or if he's just an early riser, but I'm careful not to startle him.

"Hi, Mister Jackson. Can you help me pour the milk? It's too heavy."

"Sure," I reply as I lift the gallon-sized jug and pour milk into his sugary cereal. "Why are you awake, Noah?"

"Why are you awake?" he questions in response and I can't help but chuckle.

"Well, I have to go to work."

"Did you have a sleepover with my mom?"

I think for a moment. Noah is smart. I'm sure that he can put two-and-two together, but I don't want to get his hopes up that me and Elle may be something more.

"Would it bother you if I did?"

"No, I have sleepovers with my friends from my old house. Mom said that I could have a friend sleepover when school starts because I'll be making a lot of new friends. You're my friend, maybe we can have one giant sleepover," Noah proclaims enthusiastically.

"Maybe. We'll have to check with your mom. Now tell me what you're doing awake."

"Oh, I saw a man looking in my window," Noah says without a care as he takes a large spoonful of cereal and piles it into his mouth, milk dripping down his chin.

"What? Noah, a man was looking in your window?" This is a safe neighborhood; maybe what he saw was his imagination. "Are you sure you weren't dreaming or saw a shadow?"

"No, it was a person, but I couldn't see who it was because it was dark. They scared me, so I got out of bed and came to get breakfast. My stomach was hungry."

"Okay, little man. I'm going to take a look outside and I'll be right back, okay?"

"Don't you have to go to work?" he asks as if he's worried about my job.

"I own the work, I can have someone else open."

"Oh! You're the boss? My dad hates bosses."

Well, your dad is a douchebag, kid. But I don't say that out loud.

"I am the boss. Sit tight. I'll be right back."

I open the front door and look around finding nothing out of the ordinary but decide to take a look at the window looking into Noah's room; it's the one facing the front yard. Even though it's dark, I can see that some of the grass has been pushed down, obviously stepped on, and that has my hackles rising. Elle is here by herself and the kids most of the time; I don't like the idea of someone looking in on her.

Back inside I check the deadbolts, making sure they're secure and locked properly. I send a text to the other opening trainer and let her know that I won't be in today, then I walk over to Noah who is just finishing up his cereal.

"Hey, how would you like to go with me to the store real quick?"

"Really? Where are we going? Can I get a toy?" he asks at a rapid speed, but before I can respond he's hopping off the stool and heading toward his bedroom, I assume to get dressed.

I turn and make my way back to Elle's room to let her know what's going on, but I find myself standing at the foot of the bed staring at her. She looks stunning with her hair fanned out across the pillow, her body stretched out as she lies on her stomach, the sheet barely covering her bottom.

For a moment I'm transported back to college when I took one last look at my girlfriend, Katy, before I packed up and left. We had gotten engaged the weekend before after being together for two years. I thought she was the one, my missing half, my soul mate. We were talking about the kind of wedding we wanted, where we wanted to live, and our plans once we graduated. That night she had told me that I should look at getting a regular nine-to-five job, that opening my own business wasn't going to be feasible if we wanted to raise a family. I understood her concern, it was valid, and I spent most of the night mentally reconsidering my plans.

At midnight I had hopped on our computer, a laptop that we shared, and began searching for jobs that I could apply for, but as I ran a search for my resume document, a message popped up under her social media account. I was about to close it out but then I noticed the name at the top. It was a message from my friend Sam. He wanted to meet up with her to convince her not to marry me, he said that he loved her.

I scrolled through the message, unable to control my curiosity, and discovered that they had been hooking up behind my back for years. Years. All this time wasted. There were pictures, a lot of pictures. Pictures of him, pictures of her, pictures of them together. It was more than I could take.

I remember closing the computer and searching for a piece of paper to leave her a note. I said nothing more than goodbye and that Sam will take good care of her. Before I left I had taken one last look at the woman I had planned to spend my life with. She was resting on her stomach with her hair fanned out on my pillow. It's how she slept every night. I reached over to our dresser and grabbed the two-carat diamond ring my mother helped me purchase because I knew that Katy wouldn't want a hand-me-down. I placed it in my pocket and never looked back. The first thing I did that next morning was find a temporary apartment to last through graduation and get my money back on the ring. I was lucky that the jeweler was so understanding.

Elle says something in her sleep as she reaches out across the cold sheet and I'm brought back to now. I know Elle isn't Katy. I know she isn't going to break my heart like Katy did. It takes faith and I am going to do all I can to prove to Elle that she can have faith in me. I'm not a playboy because I want to be. I stayed away from relationships to keep from being hurt, but I'm ready now, and I believe Elle is too. She's probably been ready a lot longer than she knows.

Walking over to the side of the bed I crouch down and bring my face close to hers. "Elle," I whisper and then repeat as I try to wake her up slowly.

"Hmm?" she murmurs as her eyes flutter open. As she recognizes me, she smiles broadly amidst her sleepy haze.

"I'm going to the store and taking Noah. He's awake."

"Okay, but don't you have to work?"

"I have someone else opening. We need to have a talk, but that can wait until I get back."

"Is something wrong?" she asks, her mind coming awake at the thought.

"I don't think so. I'll make sure to lock up behind myself, and I'll grab your keys."

"Okay," she replies and I kiss her quickly before leaving the bedroom, Elle's face marred with confusion. Luckily I find my shirt in the hallway andItug it on.

Noah is waiting for me in the living room wearing a black shirt, black pants, and a Batman cape. Can't fault the kid for having awesome superhero style.

"Alright, Batman. Let's go save the world."

Noah and I return from the store about two hours later just as Elle and Kennedy are getting out of bed.

"Welcome back," Elle greets us as Noah runs into the house like he hasn't seen his mother for days. "What did you all get?"

"We'll talk about it later. How about I make everyone breakfast and you can take a bath or shower or whatever you do to relax?"

Elle surprises me as she walks over and wraps her arms around my waist and rests her chin on my chest. I wouldn't have pegged her to show this kind of affection in front of her kids, but I am not going to look a gift horse in the mouth.

"Are you suggesting I spend a non-concrete amount of time in the shower, merely soaking in the warm water, without fear that my children will run out into my asshole neighbor's yard and bug him?"

"Yes, that is what I am suggesting."

"And what about the asshole neighbor?" she asks as she raises one of her eyebrows in a mocking glare.

"He may just find a way to keep the kids entertained for a while and join you."

"Ah, yes. That would definitely be an asshole move." She rises on her tiptoes and moves her hands to my shoulders so that she can whisper in my ear. "Maybe I'll leave the door unlocked."

This sexy side of Elle leaves me speechless, and as she steps away, she trails her hand down my chest and across my cock restrained in my jeans. I hear the door click to the bathroom and I take a moment to readjust myself before turning my attention to the kids perched on the barstools.

"Alright, who wants pancakes?" I ask and I'm answered with the high-pitched squeal of the kids in acceptance.

Somewhere along the way I got flour and water all over myself, a rookie move, so I take my shirt off and ball it up to take home later. The kids are curious about my tattoos so I answer all of their questions as best as I can, always reminding them that their mom sets the rules. I'm pretty sure Elle is going to find her kids covered in marker later this afternoon.

Just as I'm plating the third doughy creation for Kennedy, the perfect shape of a particular girl mouse, a knock sounds at the door. I turn off the burner and listen for Elle, the shower is still running in the hall.

"Y'all sit tight, okay?"

"Yes, Mister Jackson," they reply in unison.

A series of knocks sound again, an urgent staccato of beats, before I can get to the door.

I open the door wide and I instantly know who is on the other side, Elle's ex-husband Dan.

His confident smile falters as he looks me over and then he grimaces as he asks, "Who are you?"

"Doesn't matter." I cross my arms over my chest, blocking his view of the inside of Elle's house.

"I want to see my daughter. It's her birthday. Where is Elle?"

"Well, that's not going to happen and her birthday was yesterday. And Elle is indisposed," I allude, loving how the man's face turns a sick shade of red.

"What are you doing with my Elle?"

"Elle is no longer your concern if memory serves."

"She's my wife!" he argues and tries to push past me, but I don't budge. Though Dan is lean and muscular, I stand about four inches taller than him and I have about twenty-five more pounds of muscle. But even if I was smaller, I am not letting him into this house without Elle's consent.

"Sir, I suggest you leave before I have to contact the police for trespassing."

"That's my wife!" he shouts as he tries to push past me again, his hand falling as he comes in contact with my chest.

"Ex."

"I don't want my children around a troublemaker like you. Before I know it they'll be joining a gang and doing drugs. I don't know what Elle even sees in you."

"Like I mentioned, she's not your concern. And you know nothing about your children or me. Now, I'm only going to ask you one more time to leave before I have to call the cops."

"You ain't calling nobody," he fumes as he stands before me with a blue bag dangling from his fingers.

Luckily, my brother has picked the perfect time to show up. He parks on the street and climbs out of his county-issued SUV and makes his way over to us. I smile over Dan's shoulder at him and he nods in understanding. We've spoken about Elle before so he's smart enough to deduce that this is her ex.

"I received a call about a disturbance. Can you tell me what's going on?" Cooper asks, but Dan just tosses the bag on the porch and stomps away.

"What was that all about?" Cooper asks, and I relay everything that happened this morning and what I perceived happened last night.

"That's a good idea about a security system. I can come by later and help you install it. Hey, shouldn't you be at work?" he asks, but I'm already backing away from him and into the house.

"No, I should be in the shower. I'll meet you at my house in thirty," I explain as I shut the door in his face.

I do believe there is a woman in the shower waiting for me.

Chapter Nine

Elle

OUR TRYST IN THE shower doesn't last too long; of course, I had already been willing and ready for about fifteen minutes. But those fifteen minutes were some of the most relaxing in my life. Even when Dan and I had a nanny, or the kids were at their playgroups, I could never truly relax. My mind was always in "mom mode," but for some reason, I trust Jackson explicitly.

After our shower, he explains how he woke to find Noah sitting at the counter eating a bowl of cereal and when he asked Noah about it he had explained that he had seen a person. I wonder if Noah made it up. But Jackson details that he had gone outside to find footprints in the dewy grass just outside the front bedroom window – Noah's bedroom window.

I want to scream and shout and move to the other side of the country. I can't even protect my babies in our own home. I pace around the living room contemplating what I need to do, but I come up with no resolution.

After I have my meltdown, Jackson shows me the security system he purchased this morning and I almost propose to him. This man. This man that I barely know and has at any given time angered me so thoroughly that I consider setting his house on fire, went out and bought a security system to protect my children and me.

"I'm going to install it with Cooper this afternoon, but I have a suspicion of who it may have been."

"You do?"

"Your ex came by this morning while you were in the shower. That is why it took me so long."

Truthfully, I had thought he needed to run next door to get more condoms.

"Dan? What did he want?"

"He came by claiming that you were still his wife and that he wanted to see his daughter and give her a birthday present."

"Hold up," I say, holding my hand up in the air for emphasis, which just causes Jackson to chuckle. "My ex-husband, who so much as didn't even call on Kennedy's birthday even though he was sent an invitation to her party, decided to show up at my house at six in the morning and demands to see my kids?"

"In a nutshell, yes," he replies. "I'm fairly certain he was peeking in the window to try and find a way inside. I want you to be careful, Elle. It seems like his head isn't screwed on too tight."

I plop down on the couch and rest my head in my hands as despair washes through me.

Why can't I just move on with my life? Why can't he just take the hint that it's over? He is the one that cheated on me and is now filling my spot with my ex-best friend Sky. What a nightmare.

"Jackson," I begin as I look up at him. My eyes follow his path as he takes the seat next to me and grasps one of my hands between his. "What am I going to do? What would you do?"

One of his rough hands reaches up and strokes the light stubble on his chin, the same stubble that left burns on my thighs in the shower. I squirm in place as I remember how it felt to have the scruff rub against my skin.

"I think," he begins, bringing me back to the moment, "that you're the mother and you know what's best for your children. I've never been a parent, so I don't think that I'll have sage advice for you. But as the brother of a cop, I can tell you that you absolutely need to bring this to your lawyer. If he is only allowed certain visitation, he shouldn't be stepping over those bounds he was given."

"You're right. I guess I should call Sara."

"Good. For now, just relax and enjoy the day. I'm going to go watch a game with my brother then I'll be back over."

"Jackson?" I say as he stands from the couch.

"Yeah?"

"Thank you," I whisper, unable to find the words needed to express my gratitude.

"You're welcome, Elle."

I watch him leave, that fantastic backside covered only in that dark denim, his back muscles bunching as his arms swing slightly with each step. God, he's gorgeous.

As a promise to Noah and Kennedy, we spend the rest of the morning watching Noah's movie from last night and making slime. I don't know what parent decided to gift Kennedy a slime-making kit, but I hope that they get a case of explosive diarrhea. This stuff goes everywhere and is impossible to clean up. But the kids are laughing as we sit out on the back deck making slime of multiple colors.

After fixing the kids some hotdogs for lunch, I join them outside with a book, waiting for Sara to arrive. I called her after Jackson had stepped out of the house and she said that she wanted to meet with me today.

I bring a book out onto the patio, a romance novel I've been dying to read for the past few months. Sara's mom had recommended it to me. Just as I open to the first chapter, I hear the kids greet Jackson and Cooper from their clubhouse. I haven't met Cooper officially yet, but as he walks beside Jackson, I can see the family resemblance. The only difference is their shade of hair color.

"So, you must be the new neighbor," Cooper claims by way of a greeting.

I stand and walk down the patio steps to address them. "That would be me. You're the asshole's brother?"

"God, I like her," Cooper claims as he teases his brother. "If you're single please let me take you out."

I can feel the blush growing rapidly on my cheeks at his request, honestly not sure if he is joking or not.

"Pretty sure she's taken, Coop," Jackson replies as he steps toward me, one of his hands sliding below my chin and tilting my face toward him to press a kiss against my lips. "Hey," he whispers against my mouth and I lose all train of thought.

"Um, hey."

We stare into each other's eyes, neither of us needing words to know what the other is thinking. The silence grows around us and from the corner of my eye I watch as Cooper grabs a bag from the table and dumps it open. But my focus isn't on him, it's on the way Jackson's eyes pierce through me seeking my deepest and darkest secrets. The way the flecks of green in his eyes mix with the blue as his gaze seeps through to my soul.

It's a heady feeling, this sensation of longing and hunger as it rushes forth. It's nothing I've ever experienced before and it leaves me almost gasping for air. I shouldn't have this reaction to Jackson, or anyone. I should be busy sorting out my life and making sure that my kids are taken care of. But in this perfect, beautiful moment as the world swirls around us, all I feel is. ..love, and that is terrifying in and of itself. I've never experienced a love that knocks you on your ass and bleeds you dry. The kind that demands everything that you have without seeking anything in return. A love that becomes such a part of you that you feel complete for the first time. That kind of love has only been the stuff of fairytales in my experience, but for some reason, I can sense that whatever is happening between Jackson and me is going to be the roller-coaster of my life. The question is if I'm ready to strap myself in.

A knocking noise sounds from around us bringing Jackson and I back into the world of consciousness, his face reflecting some of the same emotions that I'm sure are showcased on mine. We turn in unison to find Sara standing at the patio table with a smirk gracing her lips.

"Well, hello you two."

"Hey, Sara," I say as I step away from Jackson. "Have I introduced you to Jackson?" I ask, and for the first time, I actually fear what Jackson's reaction may be. Sara is gorgeous, I'm a good enough friend to recognize it and not let it worry me. Usually. But today I wait for that glimmer in Jackson's eye. That look of interest that passes on most men in her presence.

I visibly relax when I notice that the look never comes. Instead,his gaze stays focused on me, his eyes only darting toward her when I ask if they've met.

"Ah, so you're the neighbor I've heard so much about. I believe we crossed paths a while back, but we have never met officially. I'm Sara. Elle's lawyer and best friend."

"Jackson, the asshole neighbor," he claims as he reaches out to shake her extended hand just as I shake my head. I'm not ready for Sara to know about my potential relationship with Jackson. She'd end up pushing us together quicker than I can prepare a no-bake cheesecake, and I'm just coming to terms with the fact that I may actually feel something for him.

"Jackson, I need to go over some things with Sara. Do you think you could help Cooper?" I ask, blatantly steering him away from us. Luckily he nods his head and moves to the side of the house to exit the backyard.

Just as I take a seat across from where Sara stands, she says, "That was some kind of look passing between you two. Are you sure that there isn't more going on?"

The heat rises on my cheeks; I can feel it, that flood of shame as I keep a secret hidden from my best friend.

"No, he was just giving me a hard time for asking him and his brother to install a security system for me. You know, typical bully stuff."

She seems to contemplate my words and then nods as she accepts them. I almost want to ask her about Cooper since she had seemed anxious around him when we saw them in the restaurant last time, but I keep my thoughts to myself as she pulls out some paperwork from her bag.

"What are these?" I ask as she places three different piles in front of me.

She points to the stack on the left and says, "This here is your documentation of what occurred this morning with Dan visiting on a non-approved day without an invitation. It also documents how you believe that Dan was trespassing on your property during the night. I simply need you to sign it. If the judge wants to bring this to court, you'll need to complete a signed statement."

"Okay." I nod, read through the simple statement and sign, then I point to the stack of papers in the middle.

"This," she begins, "is the paperwork stating that you would like a restraining order against him for you only. We don't need to do this today. I want you to think about it, but I highly recommend issuing it. Him coming here today is not a good sign, Elle."

"How will I share the kids with him?"

"Well, that's something I also want to talk to you about. Just hang onto the restraining order paperwork for now. If you fill it out just let me know and we can talk about it, but I am concerned about him just stopping by like this. That's not something he would normally do. In our meetings he made it seem like he wasn't interested in the kids at all. Do you know if he and Sky are having trouble?"

"No, I'm not sure. It's not like I asked," I reply.

"Hmm," she murmurs. "I think we may need to speak with a few friends and family to determine if things are rocky. He may be attempting to win you back, Elle."

"That's crazy, I don't want him back. He has pretty much ruined my life up to this point."

"You may not, but what about the kids?" she asks, and my silence hangs in the air. She knows that I'd do anything for my kids, even consider going back to the man that made me feel worthless, so long as they were happy. "I just want you to remember how you felt when you found out he cheated and knocked up Sky. All of the secrets and lies, Elle. I don't want that for you, even if the kids beg."

Sara makes a great point. I had never felt so small as I did the moment I caught them walking out of the doctor's office that Monday after dropping the kids off at their playgroup. The office was the same gynecologist and obstetrician office that I used, so I knew there would only be one reason that they would be leaving together. I watched as Dan kissed Sky as she pointed at the black and white images in her hands and I remember never being kissed that way. Not until I met Jackson. The kind of kiss where you forget your surroundings and the noises around you fell away.

I didn't stay long to watch their interlude. Instead, I rushed over to Sara's office and told her what happened, what I saw. That night she went home with me to confront him and Dan only smiled smugly as he confessed to his affair.

Remembering how everything I knew crumbled around me sends shockwaves through my system. It's as if I've been transported back to that day. The nausea and fear are resting on the precipice ready to push me over the edge.

"Elle?" Sara asks as the bile begins to build in my throat. "Hey, I have good news too. Let's forget about Dan for a moment, okay? Here, take a sip of water," she suggests as she pushes an unopened bottle of water toward me. I greedily accept it.

"Now, for the good news." She joyfully bounces in her seat as she takes the first set of papers and puts them in her bag and shoves the second set in my direction. She lays out two stacks of documents from the third stack.

"What's all this?" I ask as I eye them wearily.

"These, my amazing best friend, are potential contracts."

What?

"We had spoken about it in passing, but I've been dodging phone calls like crazy asking for you to provide the desserts at a few restaurants. Since it got out that the Secretary of State loves your lemon pound cake, people are very interested."

"She does?" I ask, having no idea.

I'm glad Sara offered to deal with all of the legal jargon for my business. I should probably look at getting a business manager to handle the ancillary things that aren't a part of Sara's job, but she seems to enjoy doing it.

"Yes, she does," Sara chimes in. "Anyway, what we have here are two of the contracts I think you should consider. The first is to work with Elver's Catering. They are based out of New York and you would be supplying them your recipes to have local affiliates provide the desserts at their events. This would bring you on the national level. The second contract is to work with Beckley's Baked Goods to provide your recipes along the mid-Atlantic region at coffee shops and convenience stores across the area. Neither contract is exclusive, and we have the ability to hire out on our own. These are both great opportunities." Her excitement is palpable as she goes over the fine details, the need to find a larger kitchen, packaging, all these things I never envisioned in my future.

"Sara, I'm not sure if I'm ready for that leap. It's just me and I just like to bake."

"I know, I know. I don't want you overwhelmed. I think you have the potential to become the next Little Debbie. You're that good."

"You have all of this amazing faith in me. I wish that I had it in myself." I notice another paper off to the side and slide it into my line of sight. "What's this one?"

"This is the contract I drew up to turn your business into your own baking LLC. Your desserts are amazing but your cakes, Elle? They're masterpieces in their own right. If none of these options work for you, I want you to consider expanding here. Just some food for thought. Oh, and you may have a large order of éclairs and muffins for a corporate event downtown tomorrow. Pick up is at 4:30 a.m.," she adds and ducks her head under her arms as she awaits an act of violence.

"4:30? Goodness, Sara, how many do they need?"

I watch as she opens her phone and grimaces before telling me that they need eight hundred – of each. I'm seriously reconsidering having her as my partner.

Stepping out of my seat, I rush inside the kitchen and take inventory in my pantry of all my baked goods, most of which I am seriously lacking.

"Sara, you're on kid duty. I have to go raid all the grocery stores!" I shout from behind the glass of the sliding doors and she waves me off.

I grab my purse and exit the house quickly, stopping only to find Jackson and Cooper both shirtless as they install a camera facing the entrance to my house and the driveway.

"Wow, you guys are doing great," I say, stunned at the progress that they've been making.

Jackson steps down from the bench on the porch he was using as a step stool and looks me over with heated eyes. I haven't changed my clothes, but he's looking at me as if I'm wearing the sexiest piece of lingerie. Finally, his eyes rest on my keys dangling from my fingers.

"Where are you headed to?"

"I just had a large order come in, and I'm low on some supplies, so I'm heading to the store."

"Do you want some company?"

As much as I want to take him with me, just to have some time together, I know that if he's in my presence, I'll forget something essential, like flour or eggs.

"I wish I could, but I think I'll be quicker if I'm alone. I'll be back soon. Sara is watching the kids."

"Will I see you later?" he asks with a hint of hope and I know that I'll be neck deep in baking quicksand for the day.

"I'm not sure. Maybe?" I rise on my toes and press a quick kiss to his lips, just a peck, but I know he wishes that it was more. I can feel it in the way his lips linger. He's not alone, I wish that it was more too.

My trip to the store is not nearly as quick as I wish. I end up having to travel to four different grocery chains in the area just to the find the baking flour that I like.

But finally I'm home and throwing all of the items on the large island, sorting everything out for which items I'm preparing, when I notice a note on the counter. It's got Jackson's scrawl pressed onto the white sheet of paper, and he's telling me that he got an emergency call from Hunter and had to go take care of some things with their business. It's vague, and normally I would be reading into it more, but with the timeline I have, I don't have the time or patience to get lost in thought. Sixteen hundred items aren't going to bake themselves.

Sara stays most of the day, and I'm grateful that she loves my kids as much as I do. I've always wondered why she never married or wanted a family, but she always insists that her career comes first.

I finish baking the last set of muffins and I'm just about to start the éclairs, when the doorbell rings. The new tablet perched on my counter is connected to the security system and I can see that a man is standing at my door carrying a few bags.

I didn't order anything.

"Hello?" I say as I open the door a smidge and the young teenage boy smiles showing off a full set of braces.

"Hi, I have a delivery for Miss Knight, courtesy of Jackson Divers." He holds out a bag that smells like Chinese food. In his other hand, he holds an array of wildflowers.

"What's all this?" I ask myself, but the delivery boy must hear me.

"Seems like you have an admirer. I need to try this on the girl at school I've been wanting to ask out. But she's not nearly as pretty as you," the boy says, his voice squeaking.

I take the bags and the flowers from him and turn to find Sara ushering the kids inside with a surprised look on her face.

"The neighbor?" she asks, and I bashfully smile. She already knows the answer to that question if her saucy grin is any indication. "So what did Romeo send us?"

"Chinese," I whisper, and Sara's already knowing grin widens two-fold.

"Ah, and does someone know that my best friend's favorite food is Chinese?"

"Not that I'm aware of. Stop reading into things," I say as I try to steer the conversation away from myself and Jackson.

Noah and Kennedy are already digging through the containers to find noodles and low-and-behold there is a container of lo-mein sitting at the bottom. It seems like Jackson ordered everything on the menu, most likely not sure what we would like. It's a good thing that I can save most of these items because we'll be eating like kings for days.

"So, can we talk about. . ." Sara begins, but I cut her off with a firm, "No."

"What about. . ."

"No. We are not talking about relationships, or lack thereof, or neighbors. None of it. I just want to take a moment to eat this delicious meal with my kids and best friend. Okay?"

"Fine," she huffs as she stuffs an eggroll into her mouth.

I listen as Noah describes the adventure he and Kennedy went on today. Pirates sailing on the open seas that come across an evil octopus. Noah tells us how he was able to slay the beast and save the pirate Kennedy.

Those two and their imaginations…

Dinner is quick and soon Sara is leaving so I can get the kids bathed and ready for bed. She helped me throw the first batch of éclairs into the oven, but now as I walk into the kitchen after tucking the kids into bed, the sense of feeling overwhelmed threatens to choke me.

A few hours pass until I stuff the last éclair full of filing and place the tray in my fridge.

The clock reads 1:00 a.m. and I have yet to notice Jackson pull up to his house. I have a clear view of the road from my kitchen through the living room.

I had hoped to see him again tonight, my addiction to him growing stronger every night. While I've been baking, I've thought about his request to make things more serious, and while I'm still on the fence, I've been leaning farther on the side of being something more.

Cleaning up the mess in the kitchen, I think about how my life is changing, and it's almost as if it's leaving me behind. I'm not ready for everything to change, or at least I don't think that I am. Maybe I need to begin embracing the change, embracing the opportunities before me. Not just with Jackson, but with these catering gigs as well. There is potential to make myself known countrywide. And if I take these chances will we stay here? What if Dan fights me then and it all blows up in my face?

These are the thoughts plaguing me as I undress and slide my body into bed. I'm saved from further self-interrogations because sleep captures me quickly and takes a firm hold, drawing me into the abyss.

I feel a soft brush against my waist, just the lightest of caresses on my skin and a tingling across the area where my shorts touch my hips. I try to pull myself free from my sleepy haze, to bring myself into the moment, but it's as if I'm being held captive by my mind.

The mysterious hand skirts past the waistband of my shorts and delves underneath my panties before sinking between my legs. I can feel the moan building as the deft fingers trail against my slick folds. That moan escapes between my lips as I feel the tender touch slide into my sex. I'm lost in the sensations taking place that I don't notice the buzzing on my nightstand.

Suddenly my eyelids peel back in panic, the feeling of my own touch long forgotten.

Whew, that was close.

The delivery pick up will be here in about five minutes, and I was too lost in my dream to hear the alarm for the past ten minutes. I fumble around the room and tug on a pair of jean shorts and a loose T-shirt, not needing to impress the delivery driver.

I tiptoe to the kitchen even though my kids sleep like the dead. Pulling out my signature boxes from the pantry, I get to work piling the baked goods inside. I get about halfway before I hear a knock on the door.

"Crap," I murmur as I lick some of the chocolate left by the éclairs from my fingers and move toward the door.

I'm surprised to find a man in a business suit at my door; a very attractive man in a three-piece suit with perfectly styled hair.

"Hi," I say in surprise to find him at my door.

"Hello, I'm Mark Cambridge, CEO of Hawk Associates. I believe you have some items for me to pick up?"

I stare at him in shock, not just because I didn't expect someone of his caliber to pick up the items, but because he's just so darn good looking.

Finally, I break myself from my stupor and invite him inside after greeting him like a professional.

"Sorry, I'm just finishing up packaging them."

"My apologies for the late notice. Our assistant was in charge of the order, but it seems she didn't place it before she left the company."

"Oh, that's okay. I do well under pressure," I say, and bite my lip at my inferred meaning.

Mark offers to help me pack the last few muffins and I watch him from the corner of my eye and wonder why I don't have the same reaction to him that I do to Jackson. He's obviously gorgeous, probably one of the most attractive and self-assured men I've ever met, but I don't feel that instant spark that I had with Jackson.

"May I ask where you heard of me? Er, my desserts and baked items?" I ask as we carry a load of boxes to his large SUV.

"My mother brought home one of your pies from a fundraiser a few months back and it was delicious. My girlfriend and I have been trying to find it again since."

Girlfriend. Maybe that explains why there is no spark.

"Well, I have a website for online ordering, so feel free to order as many pies as you would like," I joke as we continue to carry boxes from the house to his car.

It takes a few more trips but finally we fill the back of his car with about forty boxes holding all of the baked items. At the door, he hands me a check for the amount plus an additional fee that he insists on paying for the short notice.

Just as he's about to leave he turns around and runs a hand through his dark wavy hair.

"I'm not sure if this is up your alley or not, but my girlfriend, well fiancée, would be thrilled if you were the person to create our wedding cake."

Excitement begins to crackle and explode like fireworks inside me.

"I haven't done a wedding cake in a long time, but I think we could come up with something. When is the wedding?"

"Not for a few more months. Maybe Victoria and I can come by to taste a few things and come up with something?"

At the mention of his fiancée, I can see his face light up and then I remember the reason I loved making wedding cakes when I first started out. Dan and my relationship had jaded me for the sacrament of marriage.

"Oh absolutely!" I exclaim. "Hold on, let me grab you a business card," I say as I step back into the house and dig through the kitchen for my set of business cards that Sara had printed up for me. Finding them, I grab one and then make my way back to Mark. "Here you go. Just send me a text or email when you have free time. I can be available whenever you need."

"Victoria is going to be so thrilled. Thank you," he says as he wraps his muscled arms around me and hugs me close.

He pulls away and then steps through the doorway with a massive smile on his face. Just as he climbs into his car, I watch as Jackson parks on the street. I wave at him, but he doesn't return my gesture. Instead, I can see his snarl even from this distance.

Mark backs out of the driveway and pulls away, the grin still on his face. Jackson remains in his car, so I step back into my house with plans to get caught up on a few orders for tomorrow.

It takes a bit longer than I expect but I hear a knock on my sliding glass doors after about ten minutes. He doesn't wait for me to open the door. Instead, he slides it open and steps through. He's lucky I was of the mind to unlock it for him when I stepped back into the kitchen.

I've laid out my order sheets but the counter is empty. I start piling the flour and eggs on top, watching Jackson from the corner of my eye as he seethes against the door. The silence becomes too much for me and I finally look in his direction after I pull out the last mixing bowl.

"Hey," I say, smiling at him but he continues to frown and my confusion takes over. I try to think back to why he would be angry at me. "Jackson?"

"I've been wracking my brain trying to come up with a way to get you to agree to take whatever we're doing to the next level. It literally keeps me up all day and night. And then I see another man stepping out of your house in the early morning, and it makes complete sense."

"What-" I begin, but he cuts me off with his hand in the air.

"I at least expected exclusivity, Elle. If you were sleeping with other men, you should have told me."

And then his assumption sinks in and I gasp in horror. How could he accuse me of sleeping around, of being with anyone else while I am with him?

I am both irate and heartbroken. Even through the trials of divorce, I have never been accused of being anything other than an honest woman.

"Get out," I say in a low voice almost startling myself. Jackson's demeanor changes at my tone and his mouth hangs open in surprise. He quickly recovers and strokes his hand through his hair then takes note of the invoice and check from Mark resting on the counter closest to him.

"What's this?" he asks as he lifts it up and his eyes widen at the amount just like mine had minutes ago. He reads over the invoice as I begin to crack eggs into the mixing bowl, ignoring the way my body tightens as he pins his gaze in my direction. I can hear the soft rustle as the papers fall back onto the counter as I pour a few cups of flour into the mixture. I measure out the sugar as he takes heavy steps toward me and rests his body against mine, his chest to my back. His arms rest on either side of me and his forehead lies on my shoulder.

"I'm sorry," Jackson says, and I can hear how much it pains him to admit it. I know enough of Jackson to know that he rarely apologizes for anything, but he also is rarely wrong.

I set the measuring cup and bag of sugar back down on the counter and turn in his arms, forcing him to raise his head. His eyes are sad and heavy, but not from lack of sleep, though I'm sure that the lack of shut-eye is attributing to his demeanor. I'm not sure why, but I have the strongest desire to wrap my arms around him, so I do. Jackson immediately responds by wrapping one arm around my waist and the other rests along my shoulder as his hand cradles my head against him.

We don't speak, words aren't needed. I hear the rest of his apology and he hears my words of distrust at his assumption. It's strange, having a silent conversation with someone and knowing that they hear and understand everything you're saying, that they're actually listening. I never had that with Dan, and whoever made Jackson this cautious about relationships deserves to have lost him.

After a few minutes, Jackson pulls back from me and looks down at me with his hands cradling the sides of my face.

"Go out with me," he commands, and the look in his eyes is hypnotizing.

"Like a date?" I ask.

"Yes, like a date. I can get my parents to watch the kids for you. Please."

I had planned on saying yes but hearing the please from his lips has me agreeing instantly.

"When?"

"Friday. I know that Noah starts school this week and you'll want to be with him."

Well just melt my heart why don't you?

"Friday. Okay."

Jackson presses a delicious kiss to my lips to seal the deal and I'm practically begging for more as he pulls back.

"I'm sorry that I wasn't here. Hunter was rushed to the emergency room and I needed to square things away and then get him taken care of."

I haven't met his cousin yet, but the mention of something happening to him makes my heart drop.

"What happened?"

The anxiety around Jackson is almost tangible as he takes a deep breath and describes what happened. Hunter had been mowing on a steep grade and the riding mower had flipped over, pinning him underneath the machine. The property owner had seen what happened and called the local fire and rescue to help and Hunter was rushed to the emergency room. Luckily he only needed a few stitches and some antibiotics for a few burns. Jackson was left to finish the other projects scheduled for the day then he went to check on his cousin.

"I'm sorry about Hunter. Is there anything I can do?"

"Can you help me hire a few people?" he jokes, but I think about Sara's brother and his friends.

"Actually, the guys that built the playset may be able to help. I can get you in touch with Sara's brother."Jackson grimaces and then nods. "And why don't you head home to get some rest? I'm sure that you're capable of working from home today."

"Yeah, you're right. I'm going to look into hiring more staff all around."

"That's smart of you."

"You should take the hint," he adds as he eyes the six orders I've laid out on the counter.

Before I can reply, he kisses the tip of my nose and then steps through the kitchen toward the door.

"Friday!" he roars as he steps outside.

"Friday," I whisper back to the empty room.

Chapter Ten

Jackson

FRIDAY COULDN'T HAVE TAKEN any longer to get here if it had been a tortoise flipped on its back trying to lose a race. Seriously, I haven't been this impatient for a date since – ever.

Cooper sits on my couch laughing at me as I roll up the sleeves of my shirt. I tried to look presentable by wearing a button-down shirt, but I'm pretty sure Elle won't care what I am wearing. I also wish that Cooper would have stayed at his own apartment and would leave me alone, but he seems adamant on making me miserable.

"How do I look?" I ask, not really wanting an answer from him. Cooper grins and winks then turns his attention back to the game on the television. So much for his help.

I check myself in the mirror by the door one last time and then look down at my watch.

"Why don't you just go over there? It's not like it's a blind date or anything."

But it's an important date. A date that I'm hoping will change her mind and give us a chance.

"Don't wreck my place while I'm out."

"Yes, Dad," Cooper mocks as I head out.

"And don't forget that Mom and Dad are next door watching the kids, so maybe check in with them, okay?"

"Got it," Cooper says as I close the door and head across the driveway.

Before I know it I'm at Elle's front door and my hands are sweating like I'm picking up my date for prom. I would never tell Elle, but I was a bit of a nerd in high school, and I am more nervous now then I was picking up my date for junior prom. She stood me up and I hit a growth spurt that summer. I was never stood up again.

I guess since I'm picking her up she can't really leave me hanging unless she refuses to answer, but I know that my parents just arrived about five minutes ago. They'd make sure she shows up, right?

Before I have the chance to knock, the door swings open and my dad stands there with a half grin looking in my direction.

"How much longer are you gonna stand there, son?" my dad asks, and I shake my head. "Come on in."

"Thanks," I reply, stepping into Elle's house and finding my mom sitting on the floor building an impressive house out of Legos. "Hey, guys."

Noah's attention turns to me immediately and Kennedy bends her head to disguise a blush that resembles her mother's.

"Are you going to church?" Noah asks, and I look at him with a furrowed brow in my confusion. "Mom makes us look nice for church."

Ah, makes sense.

"Nope, no church for me, but I'm taking your mom out to dinner," I explain as I bend to his level.

"Why?"

"Um. . ." I begin and glance at my mom who sits with her back against the couch hiding her laugh. "Well, Noah, I like your mom and sometimes when you like someone you want to do something nice for them. I want to do something nice for your mom by taking her to dinner."

"Oh, so it's like that time mom took us to the trampoline park even though she had been crying?"

I look to my mom again and see her face fall and it mimics what I imagine is on my face as well.

"Yeah, kid. Just like that."

"Okay," he says and goes back to playing with his Legos and building his fortress.

It amazes me how quickly these kids come to terms with changes in their lives.

I feel my mom's hand on my arm and I look over at her, she smiles.

"You look handsome," she whispers.

"Thanks, Mom."

As I stand up, I notice a shadow cross down the hallway and then I come face to face with female perfection. Cascading down Elle's body is a red dress that hugs every one of her delectable curves. The top dips just low enough to show some of her cleavage, but not enough to be overly revealing. The skirt ends on the part of her thighs right above her knees and as she does a little spin, I'm captivated at the way the material skims across her backside.

She fastens a pair of black strappy shoes while holding onto the corner of the wall and then stands up to fluff the soft curls of her hair. When I finally take in Elle in the full package, I'm awestruck at how gorgeous she looks. It's not just her hair, the makeup, or the dress, not even the fuck-me shoes, it's just Elle.

I must stand there mouth agape because I feel a kick against my foot and it brings me back to the moment.

Slowly I approach Elle and watch in fascination as her eyes travel up and down my body causing her cheeks to turn almost the same shade of red as her dress.

"You look beautiful," I say, as I snag her hand.

"Thank you. You look handsome."

"Thanks. Are you ready?"

"Sure," she says, and we make our way to the door, but I feel her hand slip from mine as she leans down and hugs both of her kids and reminds them to behave. Before I know it, her hand is back in mine and all is right in the world.

I take us to a restaurant on the outskirts of town hoping to keep prying eyes from interrupting our night. Both of us have a lot of clients scattered across the city, so the chance is there that we'll run into someone we know, but I try to keep it as slim as possible. The restaurant is a bit swanky and known for its seafood, but having only been here for a few months, I'm hoping that it's not someplace Elle has frequented before.

After exiting the car, I escort us inside and I give the host my name for the reservation and then we're sat in a private alcove in the back.

"This is nice," Elle says, as I hold out her chair for her to take a seat. After pushing her chair under the table, I promptly take the seat across from her.

"Have you been here before?" I ask as the server fills our glasses with water.

"No, I haven't been much of anywhere. We. . . I mean Dan and I didn't go out to eat very often."

"That surprises me. I would have bet that he wanted to show you off."

She huffs out a breath at my statement but I can tell that it's not in amusement, it's in exasperation.

"Anyway," I continue, trying to steer the date back to happier terms, "I haven't been here before either, but my parents say it's excellent."

Elle smiles and I can see her demeanor change as I mention my parents.

"They're so nice. I really appreciate them watching Noah and Kennedy."

"Believe me, you're doing them a favor. They've been harping on Cooper and me about giving them grandkids for years."

"I'm sure you've given them a lot of false hope," Elle points out referring to the few women I've bedded previously that she's encountered since we've met.

"Funny," I add as the waiter comes by to take our drink order. "So, there is something I'm curious about."

"What's that?"

"I knew James, but he never mentioned having a daughter, and at the birthday party, your parents seemed surprised at the state of the house. Want to shed some light on that?"

"I wish I could. My mom never mentioned my birth dad in conversation. I remember meeting him a few times as a child but after that, he kind of drifted away. I think my mom getting married to a political figure didn't help things. I feel bad that I never had the chance to know him or mourn his death, and I will always regret that."

The waiter returns with our glasses of wine and we each take a sip before placing our food order.

As he walks away, I take Elle's hand and say, "Well, you should talk to your mom about it. I don't think it's fair that she kept him out of your life but maybe there is an explanation. On the other hand, would it make a difference?"

"You're right, I should talk to her. If not for me, for my kids. They deserve to know about their biological grandfather."

The dinner takes a lighter note and we talk about growing up and college where Elle tells me of the antics her and Sara would get into. She tells me about meeting Sky and how they hit it off right away and how she mourns the loss of her friend. I mention Cooper, Hunter, and I growing up and causing trouble. How the school had a hard time telling us apart even though we were all different ages. I tell her about my ex that cheated on me and how torn up I was about it. How I almost didn't start my businesses to cater to her plans.

We talk about everything and nothing, and by the end of the date, we're almost the last two in the restaurant.

"This was nice," Elle says as I take her back to the car after paying the check.

"Best date I've been on. Maybe because it was with you."

"Sweet talker," she jokes as we come to the passenger side of the car.

Instead of opening the door, I spin her so that her back lands against the door and I pin her against the metal with my hips. Our mouths crash together, both of us yearning for the taste of the other. Our tongues feel and explore the other's mouth, and our hands memorize the curves of each other's bodies.

"Jackson," she whispers against my mouth as one of her legs begins to rise on the outside of my hip.

"Not here," I say, and I pull away from her, disappointment flashing in her eyes. "Get in the car," I command, and I quickly shut the door after she slips inside and I dash around the front of the car and enter the driver's side.

I turn on the ignition and place the car in gear before heading out of the parking lot. From the corner of my eye, I watch Elle squirm in her seat and that only causes my dick to harden more behind my zipper.

"I'm not ready to go home," she says boldly as she turns her head my way. "Can we go back to your place?"

"I'm not ready for the night to be over either, but Cooper is at my place. I have somewhere in mind, though."

She nods and doesn't say anything more, but I can tell she is fired up as I place my hand on her thigh and she lets out a gasp of pleasure at my touch. My fist grips at the skirt of her dress and I hike it higher on her thighs until I come in contact with her flesh. I rock my hand back and forth stroking her soft skin until Elle surprises me and places her hand on top of mine and guides it further up her thigh to the place she wants it most.

I can feel the warmth of her sex before I come in contact with it and it takes all of my strength to focus on the road ahead of me. Luckily, we don't have much farther before we arrive at the lake with a hidden parking lot that was notorious as a makeout point when I was in high school. I'm hopeful that it no longer holds that title as I don't plan to share Elle with anyone else tonight.

The turn comes quickly and I take it a bit too fast forcing me to slide my hand across Elle's bare slit. Her moan is like an angel's song in my ears. Around us, dust floats in the air as I stop on a dime and put the car in park.

"What are we doing here?" she asks, her voice husky with want.

"We're here because I'm going to fuck you senseless, Elle," I reply, my own huskiness evident to my ears.

"Oh, okay."

I scoot the seat back as far as it will go and tug Elle over to my lap where she immediately straddles my thighs.

"God, you're gorgeous," I say, running my hands up and down her sides then sliding my hands underneath the skirt of her dress. Her skin is hot, like the sand on a beach underneath the scorching sun.

Elle rocks her body against me and I'm not sure if it's the alcohol that has made her braver or the fact that we've been away from each other for the week. It was a forced solitude by me because I want to treat her right and show her that she's more to me than just a quick lay. I texted her off and on during the week, maybe even a little sexting. Elle definitely has a hidden minx beneath her mom facade.

"I've thought about this all week. Being alone with you," I tell her as she begins to rock her hips against me seeking out the sweet friction she desires.

"I've thought about you too," she says breathlessly as she tosses her hair behind her and arches her back.

"What did you think about, Elle? Tell me."

"I thought about your hands and your mouth," she pants.

Gliding my hands higher on her thighs her breath catches as my thumb caresses her soft and slick folds.

She moans into the confined space as she lets her body guide her toward her pleasure. Elle's body sways against my hand as my palm rubs circles against her clit.

"What exactly were they doing?" Using my free hand, I unfasten my pants and slide the zipper down freeing my hardening cock.

"This. They were doing this, making me feel everything. Making me want everything." Her breathing increases, and it takes only a few more twists of my hand before she's throwing her head back in ecstasy. "I need you inside me, Jackson. Now. Please," she demands, and I quickly extricate my wallet from my pants and remove the condom inside.

"Put it on me," I tell her as I place the condom in her hand. She looks at it as if she has never seen one before and then tentatively reaches out to grasp my cock with a look of confusion on her face. Suddenly I realize that she's never done this before. Covering her hand with mine, I show her how to squeeze the tip and then roll the latex down my shaft. Her smile is triumphant as she reaches the base and I would join her in her enthusiasm if the feel of her hand on my erection didn't completely unman me.

"Take what you want, Elle," I say as she hovers above me, her legs cocooning my hips underneath her body and I lay the back of the seat almost parallel to the ground.

Elle rests her hands on my chest as she rocks her hips back and forth, coating me in her sweetness, teasing herself with my cock, and driving me wild. After what feels like forever, she finally rises up and grasps my erection with her hands before slowly sliding me inside her, inch by glorious inch.

Elle lets her body settle and adjust to my size, as she pins her eyes on me, seeking a connection I'm all too happy to give.

I almost spit out those dreaded words, the three words I know would have her running for the hills. It's been a little over a month and I know for certain that I'm in love with my annoying neighbor with the long brown hair, gorgeous legs, and two rugrats.

I know that she isn't ready for me to say it, or ready for her chance to move forward, but I can guide her, make her see that if I can make a relationship work then so can she. But I will be patient, give her time to adjust to having me in her life.

"Elle, baby, I need you to move," I hiss through my teeth as her body clenches around me.

She begins to pulse up and down, just the tiniest of movements, until her body awakens with pleasure. It takes only a minute before her pace increases and she's moving my cock in and out of her body as she takes control.

"Oh God!" she cries out as the waves crest inside her sex, squeezing my cock with all their might.

I'm close, so freaking close to my release that I take hold of her hips and begin ramming her body down on my cock. Her cries fill the car as she grips my arms, holding on for dear life. My explosion is quick, only the slightest of tingling in my spine alerting me of its arrival, and I pull Elle close once I expend myself in the condom.

Our breaths are heavy and fast, and as I look around, I notice that the windows of the car are fogged up.

"Hmm. . .that was-" Elle begins, but then a knocking on the window has her startling off my lap and back to her seat, kneeing me in the balls in the process.

"Fuck!" I cry out as she apologizes over and over again.

It takes a moment for me to tuck myself back in my pants after removing the condom and put the seat back up in its right position, all while I'm trying not to cry like a baby.

The knock sounds again and I roll the window down only to come face to face with my worst nightmare – my brother.

"Having a fun night?" Cooper asks.

"Cooper," I groan, and roll my eyes at his bad cop routine.

"You know that I haven't really arrested anyone in a long time. Oh, hi there, Elle. Did you have a nice date?"

"Cooper," I reiterate, and that asshole just smirks at me. Is this how Elle felt every time I egged her on?

"Yes, Mister Divers?"

"What are you doing out here? This isn't even your jurisdiction."

"I'm here to make sure that my brother is treating his date with care and respect. And because I knew that you wouldn't be able to keep it in your pants long enough to make it home. I got a call from a local officer that your plates matched the ones turning into the park after hours. So here I am."

I grumble under my breath about baby brothers and nosy officers as Cooper leans away from the car.

"Why don't you two head on back?"

"Thanks, Cooper," Elle says quietly, and I look over to find her with her head down and her hair curtaining around her face. I hope this incident doesn't take us one step backward.

Cooper waits for me to start the car and exit the lot before he trails behind us. Just as we get on the main road, I turn to glance at Elle, and I'm surprised to see her body shaking as she covers her mouth with her hand.

"Elle," I say in the hopes of comforting her, but she turns to me and bursts out in laughter.

"Oh my gosh, I'm sorry, but that is one of the funniest things that has ever happened to me."

"Yeah," I say sarcastically, "Cooper is a real jokester."

"Come on, you don't think it's funny that he came all the way out here to cock block you?"

"No. He's lucky you were dressed or I would have been going to jail for homicide."

"Oh, don't be such a party-pooper."

Elle spends the rest of the ride asking me about some of the things Cooper did growing up to get at me. It filled the rest of our time, because even though he is my little brother, Cooper knows how to get the best of me.

I pull my car behind Elle's in the driveway because she mentioned at dinner that she has no plans in the morning. Of course I have to be up bright and early to help our new hires learn the ropes. Who has new employees start on a Saturday? Apparently, I do.

Elle stays in the car as I've asked her so that I can walk her to the door. She smiles sweetly at me as I place my hand on her lower back as we stroll up her walkway.

"Thank you for the date. It was wonderful."

"You're welcome, I enjoyed it too. But I'm going to be a gentleman and leave you here."

"Really?" she asks surprised. As if I'll let my parents know that I'm sleeping with her.

"Yes, really," I reply as I place a kiss on the cheek of her shocked face. I love the way her lips form that perfect "O" shape.

"Goodnight, Elle."

"Goodnight, Jackson," she counters, and I can hear the bewilderment swirling in her voice.

Just as I'm at the end of the walkway about to cross over to my yard I shout, "Maybe keep that window open tonight."

Her lips part to reveal a beautiful white smile and for a moment I feel like I'm blinded by the sun. I almost step back toward her, like a moth to a flame ready to be burned, but I hold steady. I don't want to embarrass her in front of my family or have to explain anything to her kids. I'll bide my time, but only for a few hours.

Chapter Eleven

Elle

THE ALARM SOUNDS ON the nightstand and I do my usual head to toe stretch as I wake, but this time I feel soreness in all of my muscles. A good soreness. The kind you get after hours of rough sex and sweet lovemaking. The kind that reminds you all day long about everything you did the hours before.

"Mmm," I moan as I stretch out my toes.

Reaching across the bed, I'm surprised to find the sheets cold and empty. I'm pretty certain that Jackson spent the night in my bed, but truthfully I had baked late into the night, and I may have dreamt him. But that doesn't explain my soreness.

He hasn't pressed me anymore about making our relationship serious, not since our date two weeks ago when his brother caught us in our post-coital bliss. I'm almost afraid that he's given up on me, but he's been just as busy as I have. With Hunter out of work, Jackson has had to step up with the lawn business in the meantime. And he's training employees night and day at the gym as well. Luckily, he took my advice and contacted Sara's brother to join the lawn team, and as far as I know everyone has been a good fit.

Finally, I swoop my body out of bed and throw on a pair of cut off sweats and an oversized T-shirt. Today is Saturday and I promised the kids we would go to the park before the weather starts to cool down. So while I'm all caught up on my baking needs for the weekend, I still like to get up early and have some time to myself.

The darkness has yet to give way to the daylight, so as I make my way down the hall I'm surprised to see light pouring in from my kitchen. I stop dead in my tracks when I notice Jackson standing in the kitchen in front of the coffee maker. His broad and muscled back is to me and I lose all train of thought as he turns around holding two coffee mugs. My focus is completely on the way his jeans hang low on his hips showcasing that remarkable V pointing down to one of my favorite parts of him.

"You're up." He steps closer to me, sealing his lips against mine in a chaste kiss before pulling back and handing me a mug full of the sweet nectar. "I was going to bring you coffee in bed."

"Oh, that was sweet of you," I finally say as my thoughts return to me. "But since we are both awake, do you want to sit outside with me and watch the sunrise?"

"Yeah, that sounds nice. I have to head to the gym soon to open, though. That's why I was up."

He takes my hand and we walk outside to sit on the patio. The sun is just peeking over the horizon, washing the sky in a pale blue. We don't speak, both of us equally as silent as the wildlife still hunkered in their nests and dens, but as the sun begins to rise in the sky, the birds come alive and awaken the world.

Taking a sip of my coffee, I turn to Jackson and say, "I've been meaning to talk to you about something."

"What's that?" he asks as he leans back in the chair, cup long forgotten.

I fidget with my fingers for a moment, not sure how to broach the question. I toss around a few thoughts in my head but decide to just ask him straightforward.

"What are we doing, Jackson? Is it still just sex? Do you still want more?"

He smirks at me in that way that usually melts my panties right off, but today I find it irritating.

"Stop smiling at me like that. I want an answer," I lash out.

"Sweetheart, we're doing whatever it is you want to do. I want to be with you, you know that. I'm just giving you some space to decide for yourself."

"Oh," I whisper, and I turn away from him and look down at my thighs. Of course, he has the perfect answer. He hasn't been distant on purpose, he's merely biding his time until I come around. It's something I've been tossing around in my head for the past two weeks.

Am I ready to move our relationship forward? Is my heart ready? And I'm already considering our demise. I have nothing to offer Jackson, just a crap ton of baggage. An ex-husband who seems to pop in whenever he feels like it, a business that demands almost all of my free time, and two kids that my world revolves around.

"Don't worry, Elle. I'm not giving up on you," he mentions as he stands from the chair and kisses the top of my head. "I've got to head to work. I'll see you later, okay?"

"Yeah."

I watch his long strides pass between our two yards and I wonder if we'd ever be in this position if I hadn't knocked down that middle fence. If we would have given each other the opportunity to let the other in.

It's hard to say. I'm almost curious if my dad played a part in us coming together. The fence surrounding each of our homes is pristine, but the one in the center was as rotten as a condemned home when I moved in.

He waves to me one last time before entering his house and I blow a kiss his way which he dramatically catches and pretends to put in his pocket.

The morning passes quickly, and around lunchtime the kids and I are sitting on a bench at the park with our picnic laid out on the table in front of us. Sara is meeting us here for lunch and she wants to go over a few things with me. That seems to be the case whenever I see her nowadays.

Just as I'm unwrapping the sandwiches for the kids, I see Sara stroll across the park in a pair of jeans shorts, a T-shirt, and Converse tennis shoes. Everybody at the park gives her a second glance as she passes because even in casual attire she is just that stunning.

"Hey guys," she says to my kids and then to me as she takes the seat across from me beside Noah.

"Hi, Auntie Sara," Kennedy replies as she stuffs her sandwich in her mouth.

"Hey," I say quietly as she settles in beside Noah and snags one of his carrot sticks. "What's this good news you have to share?"

"Well, do you remember about a month ago that I mentioned a promotion I was up for?" She waits for me to nod before continuing. "Well, I got it! I'm now a senior partner at the firm."

"Oh, Sara. I am so happy for you. You've worked so hard for this."

"I know. And now I can delegate the clients that I want to take on. Man, this is such a relief."

"Are you going to be able to go with me to New York on Monday for the meeting with Elver's?"

"Oh, shoot. I completely forgot. That's when I get my first chance to sort through clients and learn what the other junior partners are working on. I'm so sorry, Elle."

"That's okay. I can manage on my own."

"Why don't you see if your mom wants to go? Or maybe that hunky neighbor next door."

I haven't said anything to Sara about my relationship of sorts with Jackson. I'm not sure why I'm so hesitant. We've told his brother, and by now his parents know, but for me, telling Sara makes it real. And I'm not sure if I'm ready for real yet.

"I think I'll be fine, but I'll ask around, okay?"

At least I have transferable plane tickets.

Sara apologizes again while the kids and I finish up our lunch, and then we sit and watch Noah and Kennedy playing on the playground while she tells me about one of the new partners that just joined the firm. He's our age and single, which is about all of the information Sara needs.

I notice that she seems distracted though as she talks about him, as if she's forcing herself to feel this way about a stranger. It makes me think back to the moment in the restaurant so many weeks ago when Jackson and his brother had passed by our table. How she had mentioned that he seemed familiar to her, as if she naturally responded to him. I wonder if there is more to Sara and Cooper than they are letting on. But who am I to try and navigate their secrets when I'm harnessing some of my own?

"Hello, Elle," I hear a deep voice say from behind me, and I immediately reach out and grip Sara's arm, never taking my eyes off my kids playing across the way from me.

"What do you want, Dan?" I ask behind gritted teeth.

"Why don't you go make yourself useful somewhere else, Sara, while I talk with my wife."

Sara turns in her seat and from the corner of my eyes I can see that she's giving him a glare known to make bigger men cower in their places.

"I will be staying right here, Dan, with your ex-wife. And you can bet your ass that I will be sending a report of this to the judge."

"You do that. Because I also plan on sending in documentation that Elle has been placing my children in harm's way."

"How have I been doing that, Dan?" I seethe at his accusation, my pulse pumping faster in my veins.

"I've seen a man leaving your house. A man covered in tattoos and he's in their presence at all times of the day and night. He's a troublemaker. Probably dealing drugs or something like that. He's just using you, Elle."

"Jackson is not a troublemaker, he's a business owner and my neighbor. Now please do as Sara says and be on your way. You're not wanted here. Go be with your new family, Dan. We're better off without you," I add, and finally turn around to look him in the eye.

He looks disheveled, like a shell of the man I had married. His eyes are sunken in, his clothes misshapen and hanging off his leaner body, and his dominant swagger is far removed.

"What happened to you, Dan?" I whisper, not really wanting an answer from the man that overturned my life but concerned just the same.

"Sky left me, and she's due any day now," he replies, the heat leaving his voice.

"Well, I wish you both the best and that you can sort it out. Move on with your life, Dan. I have."

I'm surprised that he nods his head once and then slumps away, his shoulders lowering with every step. I almost feel bad for the way I spoke to him. We were together for years, but I have moved on with someone that treats me better than I ever expected.

"Sara, I'm going to pack up the kids and head home."

She nods and then helps me clean up the picnic leftovers before grabbing me in a hug. "Please consider the restraining order."

"I will," I say as I call out Noah and Kennedy's names and we head home.

As I pull into the driveway, I notice Jackson standing on his front porch with Cooper, and Bailey sits quietly at their feet.

"Look, Mommy, it's Bailey! Can we go play?"

"Well, let's ask Bailey's daddy first, okay?"

Both kids nod their heads and wait patiently for me to unstrap them from their seats and then they're off like a rocket soaring through the sky. Before I even have a chance to grab the bag and my purse from the seat, they're already rolling around on the ground with the dog.

"You're really making it hard to not get them a puppy, Cooper," I say as I walk up to them on the porch. "Did they at least ask you to play with her first?"

"They did. Thanks for watching her again, Jackson. I'll grab her on Tuesday."

"No rush, you know Bailey is my girl. Just don't tell Elle," Jackson fake whispers and then winks in my direction.

We watch as Cooper strolls back to his car and then heads down the road before I turn back toward Jackson who is intently watching the kids play with Bailey.

"Jackson," I whisper, and he finally turns to face me as I wrap my arms around his waist. It's the most public display of affection I've had with him and the surprise in his eyes is quickly masked by delight.

"Hey, babe."

"I have a question for you."

"Yeah, what's that?" he asks as he leans toward me, punishing my mouth in one of his heated kisses. Jackson always kisses me like I'm the last drop of water in the desert and I secretly hope that it never stops.

"You know that I'm leaving for New York on Monday and I know that you're watching Bailey, but. . . would you want to come with me?"

Jackson's eyebrows shoot up in shock and then he smiles. God, it's that magnificent panty-melting smile that can bring a woman to her knees, and I nearly fall to the ground. Thankfully my arms around his waist are keeping me upright.

"Are you saying that I get two whole days with you and two nights?"

"Yep."

"You can bet your ass that I'll be there."

We stand smiling at each other like a couple of love-struck teenagers for who knows how long, the only reason we pull apart is because Noah screams that Bailey is pooping in the grass.

"I'll text you all the information and get the ticket changed over to you," I tell Jackson as I step away and gather my kids. Something about moving away from him feels wrong, but I can't pinpoint why.

"Okay."

The kids and I make it about halfway to our house before I hear his deep voice yell, "Elle!" He waits before I turn around before adding, "Thank you."

And I really need to teach my kids how to mop because I'm now a melted puddle on the stone pathway.

Chapter Twelve

Jackson

"OH, JACKSON. YES, RIGHT there," Elle cries out in our empty hotel room. We just finished checking into the room after our flight was delayed, twice. Elle and I were tired, irritable, and hungry. But being in such close proximity for the last four hours made us hungry for something else.

Her body is resting against the wall as I pound into her repeatedly, making sure to steer clear of the suitcases across from us. We barely made it into the room before we threw ourselves at each other.

"Fuck, I'm coming, Elle," I cry out as she nips at my neck. Her fingers claw at my back underneath my shirt and my cum surges into the condom not long after she reaches her own release.

Her body slinks against me and I carry her to the bed where I quickly deposit her onto the soft duvet.

"Can we just have an entire two days of me and you in this bed?" I ask her as her heavy-lidded eyes look me over.

"I wish, but my meeting is in an hour and I need to get ready," she reminds me.

She had to call and reschedule the meeting from lunchtime to later this afternoon when our flight continued to get pushed back.

"Fine."

Reluctantly I pull away from her and begin pulling our suitcases further into the room so that she can get dressed for her meeting. Elle explained to me during the flight about Elver's catering and how they want to use her recipes for some of their affiliates. She and Sara both seem excited about it. I'm glad that Sara will be calling into the meeting though, so that Elle has someone on her team to guide her.

From the corner of the room, I watch as she strips herself of her shirt and bra, her panties and stretchy pants long forgotten on the floor by the entry. Elle opens her suitcase and pulls out a handful of lace and places it on the bed. A black garter belt, silk stockings, and a lace bra glare at me from their perch on the white duvet. My focus should be on Elle's naked body, but instead, I find it set on the luxurious material she's about to put on her body.

She reaches out and grabs the garter belt, hooking it around her waist and then doing the same with her bra. My mouth grows dry watching her put the sumptuous items on her porcelain skin. One of her legs bends and her foot settles on the bed as she takes one of the stockings in her hands. Slowly, so fucking slow, she rolls it up her leg, taking her sweet time to bring it up to her thigh where she hooks it onto her garter belt.

Am I having a heart attack? I feel like my heart is pumping my blood through my system so fast that I can't catch my breath.

Elle repeats the motion with her other leg and stocking until both of her legs are clad in black.

"Can you hand me the outfit from the garment bag?"

Wordlessly I follow her command and I walk over to the chair where I placed the garment bag. Inside I find a black skirt and a bright pink blouse made of the softest silk. It reminds me of the kind of woman Elle would have been before she met Dan. She mentioned before how she was crawling through the ranks in her career when she met Dan and then became a homemaker. I'm not disappointed at the turn she has taken, but I could tell that she had been.

As I hand her the hangers holding her clothes, I take in her body barely covered in the lace and silk. She smirks in my direction as she takes the hangers from me and I swear that I fall more in love with this confident woman.

It doesn't take long for her to finish getting ready, her makeup is simple, and she's pulled her hair in a twist at the back of her head, but she still looks like my same Elle.

"Good luck today, sweetheart."

"Thanks," she says as she wraps her arms around my neck. "Are you going to be okay all by yourself?"

"I'm sure that I can keep myself entertained. Do you think the hotel has Pay-Per-View?" I joke and she laughs, those small worry lines from earlier quickly replaced. She hasn't mentioned that she's nervous about this meeting, but I know she is. This meeting can put her business on an entirely new path.

"You're funny."

"Don't worry, I'll be fine. Go knock 'em dead."

"Thanks."

Her bottom sways with each heeled step as she moves toward the door and then an urgency rushes up inside me, and I know if I don't say something now then I'll regret it.

"Elle," I call out, and she peers at me from over her shoulder. "I love you."

Time stands still as she lets my words wash over her. The small hitch in her breath is the only indication that she hears me. I know that my words aren't a revelation for her, she has to have known by this point that I was falling deep for her. How could anyone not?

"Thanks, Jackson," she whispers behind a smile and then exits the room.

I won't lie to myself, I'm a bit disappointed that she doesn't say it in return, but I know that she'll say it in her own time. Elle reminds me of that little seed we used to have to grow in elementary school. Weeks and weeks of nothing while the seed sprouted deep in the soil with the roots twisting and expanding until the ground has had enough and then a beautiful flower would blossom from the tiny seedling. Elle reminds me of that seed. She burrows her emotions deep inside, letting the roots fester and grow until she's overcome by them and shares them with the world.

Neither Elle or I have been to New York before, so I call down to the concierge desk and ask for some recommendations for a day trip and two dinners. Half an hour later I've got reservations for Elle and I and a full tourist day planned for us.

Elle had planned to be at the Elver's headquarter for about four hours, so I head downstairs and make my way down the busy street. The hotel we're staying at is in walking distance to a bunch of restaurants and shops. Kind of what I always imagined New York to look like.

A small shop catches my eye, and then soon my sense of smell, because as I stop in front of the door the aroma of chocolate is so enticing that I can't help but walk inside. An older woman mans the counter and finishes checking out a customer before she turns her attention to me.

"What can I help you with, young man?"

"I don't know. What do you recommend?"

"Well, that's a loaded question. I would recommend something different for everyone depending on their personality. Tell me about yourself."

"Well, I'm in love with a beautiful woman that has two amazing kids and I'm trying to get her to give me the time of day."

She blinks at me a few times, and at first, I think that I'm being set up, but then she smiles warmly and heads behind the front of the store saying that she'll be right back. It takes just a moment but she exits holding a small white box.

"This is my specialty. White and dark chocolate swirl with bits of hazelnut. Two different flavors mixed together with a little extra helping of deliciousness."

"Wow, it sounds great."

"There are two in the box. One square for you and one for your lady love."

"Thank you. How much do I owe?" I ask as I glance toward the register.

"Oh, those are on the house. I don't ever charge for love."

I start to question her but then she gives me that look. You know the one you always got growing up when you were about to say something smart back to an elder and you had to visibly keep yourself from shaking because they could see into your soul? Yeah, that look. And the woman in this chocolate shop gives a mean one.

"Thank you. I'm sure we'll both enjoy it."

"Come back and see us."

As I head out of the door, I wave goodbye to the woman manning the counter and step out into the bustle of New York. But instead of feeling squished and trampled by the people pushing and shoving their way down the sidewalk, I feel a sense of calm. My breath is steady and slow, and my mind is clear.

I turn to head back to the hotel but a sign across the street catches my eye and I move to the crosswalk to head in that direction. A bell dings as I walk in and I take in all of the items around me, lost in a world I'm completely unfamiliar with.

"Sir, how can I help you today?"

And then I launch into the same story that I told the chocolatier.

One hour later I'm strolling back into the hotel lobby with two small bags dangling from my fingers. I've stayed at high-end hotels before when I travel for conventions but nothing like this. The floor looks like It's been painted in gold and the columns in marble. It's exquisite but not more so than the woman strolling toward me from the elevators.

Elle has a broad smile on her face and a skip in her step so I know that her meeting went well.

"Hey, how did it go?"

"It went amazing. They're open to all of my ideas and know exactly what they're looking for. I just have to discuss a few things with Sara about my recipes."

"I'm so happy for you."

"Thanks. Now what do you have there?" she asks as she tries to sneak a peek into the bags.

"One is for now and one is for later."

"Hmm. . .I smell chocolate."

"Are you done with work?" I question as I wrap an arm around her waist.

"I am," she whispers, and I tilt my head slightly to press a kiss against her lips.

"Great. I have some plans for us then." I escort her back up to our room where I show her how proud I am of her accomplishment for the day.

We take a taxi to the restaurant recommended by the concierge for dinner and I give Elle the chocolates that I snagged earlier for dessert.

A carriage ride through Central Park shows us the New York nightlife, but nothing compares to the sparkle of the lights from the window in our hotel room as they bounce off of Elle's skin in the darkness. Her body looks like a series of fireworks as the lights twinkle in the distance.

The next day I get us up early and start by taking a double-decker tour bus through the city and then waiting in line to go to the 86th floor of the Empire State Building. We finish the day with a viewing of the 9/11 Memorial and Museum. Neither of us feels celebratory enough to continue our ventures after the Memorial, so we head back to the hotel and order some room service.

Before we know it our mini vacation is up and we're at the airport about to board our plane.

"I had a really great time, Elle. Thank you for bringing me," I tell her as we take our seats.

Since our dinner, she's been overly flustered, more than her usual self. I've tried to label it as being excited about her new business venture, but the longer it lasts, the more I fear that it may have something to do with me.

I'm usually not a talker, I like things to work themselves out, but the way Elle has new feelings inside me blossoming, it has my mind in a swirl.

"Hey, if it was too much for you I can back off when we get home. Give you some time to yourself," I suggest even though that is the farthest thing from what I want to do.

"No!" she shouts, startling the passengers across from us. "No, this has been the best two days of my life."

"Well, you've just seemed different, that's all. I was going to give you-"

"Time? I don't want time, Jackson. I just want you. I loved being alone with you these past couple of days. They've been the best. God, I love you, Jackson, okay? I do, and that scares the crap out of me, and I don't know what to do with these feelings."

I cut her off with a kiss. Not just to shut her up, but because if I don't do something now, then I'll most likely carry her off to the bathroom to join the mile high club.

"Those are the best words I've heard in years."

"Don't you have something else to say?" she whispers against my lips and I can't help but smile when I say, "I love you too."

As our plane touches down our hands never pull apart. Our fingers stay intertwined through the landing, baggage claim, and Uber pick up. Anyone looking at us would think that we're a new couple in love and that is a unique experience for me – being a part of something so humbling.

"What should I tell the kids when we get back?"

"You tell them whatever you're comfortable with," I say as I help her into the car. "I just don't want us to be a secret anymore."

"I know. I don't either. I just don't want to confuse them."

"I think they'll be fine, they've been around me enough."

The Uber drops us off in front of Elle's house and Sara steps out from the front door with Elle's parents. Elle had called once we boarded the plane to let them know we were heading home.

"Well, well, well," Sara calls out as I exit the car and rush around to open the door for Elle. "Look what the lovebirds dragged in."

I look down at Elle's face and I'm expecting her to roll her eyes or hunker back into the shadows of the car, but instead, I'm awarded a gleaming grin and her hands on both sides of my face before she tugs my head down to plant her lips against mine.

A catcall cries out from the direction of my house and I pull away from Elle to find Cooper leaning against my porch railing with a smug grin on his face, but he isn't looking at us. He's looking at Sara's reaction. Of course, she rolls her eyes and heads back inside with Elle's parents.

"I have one more question for you before our little vacation officially comes to an end. Would you go with me to my parents' anniversary party next week, as my date?" I ask.

"I would be honored to be with you, Jackson."

Chapter Thirteen

Elle

I'M PUTTING THE FINAL touches on Stan and Naomi's cake just as Jackson walks into the kitchen from the back porch. He whispers a hello in my ear and I practically melt at the feel of his breath against my neck.

Since we arrived back home a few days ago, our relationship hasn't changed much, but we did tell Noah and Kennedy that Jackson would be around more. I even gave him a key to my place.

I never expected to feel a weightlessness after telling him that I loved him, but the burden of trying to hide my emotions must have been taking a toll on me. Even Sara says that she can see a change in my demeanor since I've returned from my meeting with Elver's Catering.

Sara and I are still tossing around the idea of selling my recipes to the group. It will mean a lot of income for me but then I will no longer be able to produce the recipes under my own name, and that's been the hardest pill to swallow.

Just as I'm piping my last flower on the two-tiered cake and remember how fondly I enjoyed making special occasion cakes, I hear clicking of shoes on the hardwood floor and then I'm assaulted by a pair of arms around my legs.

"Mommy, look! I'm a princess," Kennedy murmurs with her mouth pressed against my knee-length chiffon skirt.

"Yes, and you look beautiful. Which princess are you today?" I ask as I take in the color scheme of the dress I laid out for her. We're going through a Little Mermaid phase, so her dress is green and purple.

"I'm Ariel!" she proclaims as she pulls away and swirls in a circle letting the skirt of her dress puff out.

"Well, you make a beautiful mermaid, sweetie."

"Thanks, Mommy. When can I have cake?"

"When we get to the party."

"How much longer will that be?" she follows up, but I'm saved as Jackson steps through the sliding doors and garners her attention. "Jackson!" she shouts, leaving me in the dust and wraps herself around Jackson.

"Hi, princess. Don't you look beautiful?"

"Thank you," she says behind a splattering of blush on her cheeks.

Jackson glances over at me with that look in his eyes that brings me to my knees just as Noah rounds the corner.

"Are you wearing a tie too?" Noah asks as he messes with his small clip-on that I put over a collared shirt for him to wear. "I'm not, but your buddy is," I say just as he rounds the corner, his eyes lighting up instantly when they fall on Jackson.

"Are you all ready to go?" I ask, slipping my feet into my sandals that I placed by the back door.

We pile into my SUV, the cake safely secured in the back, and head downtown for Jackson's parents' anniversary party. They're celebrating forty years together. When we arrive Stan and Naomi greet us warmly, especially the kids, who get love and affection poured on them in spades.

As I bring the cake into the venue Naomi's eyes light up like the fourth of July.

"Wow, you outdid yourself, Elle," Stan tells me as Jackson and I carry the cake inside and place it on the small dessert table. I take a peek at Naomi and she has moisture pooling along her lower lids and a smile painted along her lips.

"Thanks."

The concoction is two tiers of almond cake with raspberry filling. I covered it in white buttercream icing and created gum paste flowers to cascade down one side. The flowers may be my favorite part. They're white with just a hint of pale pink along the edges.

I step back as some of the Diver's closest friends marvel at my creation, a few even asking how they can order one as well.

By the time the party is in full swing the cake has been devoured, two pieces eaten by Jackson himself who said he was eating my slice too. I rarely eat anything that I make. I'm glad I had the forethought to leave some business cards at the table and with Naomi; her guests have been snatching them up left and right. By the sounds everyone had been making as they ate the cake, I am assuming that they all enjoyed it.

The party is reminiscent of a small wedding reception and I can't say that I'm disappointed. Cooper and the kids have been keeping themselves entertained by playing a mean game of hide-and-seek. Noah seems to be winning.

I'm going to have to thank Cooper later for taking the time to play with my kids. All Noah talked about during the dinner is how he wants to be a police officer like Uncle Cooper. From my vantage point beside Jackson at our table, I can see Noah duck underneath a small alcove on the stage. Cooper will be searching for him for hours.

"Are you having fun?" Jackson asks as he leans back and rests his arm against the back of my chair.

"I am. Your family and their friends are so nice. And they've all been amazing with the kids."

"Your kids make it easy. And how could anyone not love you?"Jackson adds just as the DJ calls over Stan and Naomi to dance.

A song by Billy Joel begins to blare through the speakers, "Just the Way You Are," and the couple moves in unison to the melody.

A shiver passes across my body as Jackson presses his lips against my ear. "Dance with me," he states rather than asks, and I would be a fool to say no.

His chair scraps against the linoleum as he stands up and offers me his hand which I gladly accept. As we approach the dance floor Jackson's parents smile over at us, his mom's gaze lingering a bit longer than Stan's, before they turn their attention back to one another.

Jackson's hand presses against my back, pulling me as close as possible, as one of my arms rests against his bicep, curving up toward his shoulder. Our other set of hands stay clasped together and nestled between our bodies.

The rest of the crowd fades away as Jackson and I slip into our own world. The heat from his hand sears my skin beneath my dress. He can ignite me with a single touch and it's only become more pronounced the longer that we've been together.

"Thank you for coming with me tonight," Jackson says as he spins us around the floor. I didn't know Jackson could dance but I shouldn't be surprised, he can do almost everything with skill and finesse.

"Thank you for taking a chance on me," I whisper back.

A look detonates in his eyes and I recognize it as desire. Just when I think he's going to bend down and kiss me, I feel two sets of spindly arms wrap around our legs.

"We want to dance too," Noah and Kennedy cry out as they cling to our legs and try to sway with us.

Instead of getting upset by them interrupting our moment, something Dan would have done, Jackson releases my hand and softly cradles Noah's head while gazing down at the two mood-breakers. The DJ must recognize our desire for another slow song and he doesn't disappoint.

We continue to rock back and forth to the beat, the kids clinging to us with the full force of their grip. I worry that Jackson may be feeling overwhelmed by their attention so I begin to pull back but his grip on my waist tightens. Jackson turns his face back toward me and I'm surprised by his expression – love, so much love shows in his eyes. I can't pull away from his stare to take in the full effect of his smile because I'm entranced at the light sheen covering his irises.

"Thank you, Elle," he whispers, trying to mask the gravelliness of his voice. I know that he's not seeking a response; it's not that kind of statement. He's thanking me for giving him this opportunity, a chance to have a family, to be a part of our family.

It doesn't take long before the party begins to wear on the kids, both trying their hardest not to fall asleep in their chairs, so Jackson and I decide to head back home.

Kennedy is sleeping soundly in my arms with her head burrowed against my neck and Noah is in Jackson's arms. Naomi and Stan notice us leaving and they rush over.

"Thank you so much for inviting the kids and me," I tell Naomi after congratulating them on their anniversary.

It was sweet to watch them today. They always seem to be touching each other or giving each other looks. It reminds me of what you imagine a fairytale couple growing older to emulate. It's what I had envisioned when I got married to Dan. But now? Now that vision is clouded with images of Jackson and me, and that thought doesn't scare me nearly so much anymore.

"We're so glad you were able to join us. And that cake? It's all anyone is talking about," Naomi says and Stan jumps right in, "You have a talent. You should think about exploring that more."

I nod because that's exactly what I've been doing. For the past two days Sara and I have been going back and forth with what decision to make – stay small or take it wide. My decision thus far has been swinging like a pendulum every hour.

"Thank you. I appreciate that." Kennedy snuggles closer to me and I run my hand gently down her back as Naomi looks on. I can see the yearning in her eyes, her desire to have grandchildren. Her eyes veer over to Jackson with the same look and then I see a gigantic smile grow on her face.

Suddenly she launches herself at Jackson and hugs him tightly, and he adjusts his hold of a sleeping Noah to keep him from being startled. She speaks softly to him, words I can't determine, then she's pulling back and going into the arms of her husband.

"This has been the best party," she tells Stan, and I have to agree, whoever planned this event did a remarkable job.

"Well, we'll be seeing you tomorrow," Jackson reminds them as he wraps his arm around my shoulders, pulling my side against his body. Their family cookout is tomorrow at Jackson's house.

Jackson helps me load the sleeping kids into the SUV and then he offers to drive back to my house. An offer I gladly accept because my feet are killing me in these heels.

We get the kids inside without even the slightest of hints that they're awake – a parenting feat at its finest. Just as I finish tucking in Noah and shutting his door, I turn around to see Jackson standing behind me waiting.

"Hi," he says as he wraps his arms around my waist.

"Hi," I reply, and suddenly I'm nervous. A question so insignificant sits perched on the tip of my tongue, but it's something I've been wrestling with for days.

"What's on your mind? I can see the gears spinning," Jackson jokes, and I giggle because he knows me so well.

"I've never asked anyone this before," I begin and his eyes instantly light up in excitement. "Do you want to stay the night and have breakfast with us in the morning?"

The sparkle in his eyes diminishes only slightly, but maybe it's due to the grin moving across his lips. Jackson has never been in the house when the kids wake up outside of that one time when Noah happened to be awake on his own. So this is a big step for me, letting the kids see us together in my house in the morning.

Jackson grabs my hand and tugs me toward my bedroom. I couldn't stop him if I tried, my body is completely spellbound by him, and it has been since he pounded on my door all those weeks ago.

He quickly makes work of removing my dress and then he does the same with his own clothes until we're both naked in my bed as he begins to worship my body.

And worship it he does.

I wake to the sunlight pouring through the curtain, casting beautiful rays of light on all of Jackson's muscles. Leaning up on my elbows I peer down at him. He's resting on his back with an arm tossed across his stomach, the sheet pulled low enough to barely cover his hips. Luckily we had the forethought to put clothes on before we fell asleep last night.

"I love you," I whisper, not caring if he can hear me or not. Of course, he instantly turns onto his side and uses his arm to pull me closer.

"I love you too. How much longer do you think we have?" he asks as he snakes his hand in my hair and pulls my mouth toward his in a kiss.

"A minute," I whisper against his lips. "Two max."

I'm wrong. Our quiet only lasts about thirty seconds before Noah and Kennedy come barreling into the room shouting Jackson's name as they bounce on the bed and find him there. Jackson tackles Kennedy as she looks at him like he's her prince charming and Noah wraps his arms around Jackson's neck to save his sister. I can't help but laugh at their antics.

Jackson has that look on his face, that one you see when someone has gotten their wish, that look when a child has chocolate for the first time, or when they're finally able to ride a bike without training wheels. That look of utter contentment. I have to quickly wipe away my tears of happiness, because throughout all the turmoil I've endured this year, nothing could have prepared me for how I would feel knowing that I'm the reason someone has that look.

As they continue to wrestle in the bed, I slip out and head toward the kitchen to make breakfast. Jackson has been training his new staff to take over the weekend shifts he had been manning, and this is his first weekend free, so I'm hoping to make this morning as enjoyable as possible.

As I mix some eggs for some omelets, I think about how incredible it felt to fall asleep in Jackson's arms and for him to be there when I awoke. Everything just seemed – right. Like he belongs here, with me.

I start making the omelets, tossing in a few vegetables for Jackson and me and some cheese for the kids. Just as I plate the breakfast, Jackson and the kids pour out of the hallway fully dressed.

"Wow, if all it takes for you to get dressed in the morning is having Jackson here, then we'll have to do it again," I joke, and Jackson freezes for a split second. No one else would notice, but I do. I hope he knows that I'm only kidding, even though I have been tossing around the idea of having him move in with us. That's why last night was such a big step for me.

"I like when Jackson stays over," Noah says, and Kennedy immediately shouts her agreement.

"Why is that, kiddo?" I ask.

"Because you wake up happy. And when you're happy, I'm happy. At least that's what my teacher says, I think."He ponders for a moment, his finger tapping his tiny chin.

Luckily I'm saved from having to steer the conversation because Jackson asks Noah about the epic water gun battle they're planning for this afternoon. The summer air is starting to cool so it will be a nice treat to hang out and enjoy the warmth before the season changes.

"Well, I guess we need supplies for this epic battle, right?"

Everyone agrees, even Jackson, who I am pretty sure is as excited as Noah.

We spend about an hour at the superstore and each of us picks our battle weapons. Jackson and Noah have the largest water guns, of course.

Jackson asks if he can set up the yard for the fight and not knowing that it takes so much skill and strategy, I readily agree. While he does that I get the kids in their swimsuits and then I do the same, and pull on a large T-shirt to cover myself.

When we step outside, I take in the entire two yards in amazement. In about fifteen minutes Jackson has set up two water sprinklers, water loading zones, and base, which he describes as a place to take a break.

"You and Cooper gave your mother a heart attack on a daily basis, didn't you?" I ask as he jogs over to us wearing a pair of low slung swim trunks. He notices my attention on his body and he smirks at my reaction.

"Yes, we did," he replies before kissing me quickly then handing the kids their water guns.

He instructs each of us to head to a corner of the yard and not to move until he counts down.

"Three. . . Two. . . One. . . Go!" he shouts from the other side of the yard against the fence.

In the span of five seconds, I'm thoroughly soaked from the sprinkler and Noah's incredible aim. He and Jackson have started teaming up on me and before I know it I'm slipping and sliding in the mud all while laughing like I haven't done in years.

We head over to the refueling station, and just as I'm stepping away, I slip in a puddle and fall down to the ground, yanking Jackson with me as I go. He rests his body on top of me, shielding me from the water spurting from the sprinkler.

I gaze up into his soft blue eyes, his hair curling around his face from the water, and I can easily say that I've never been in love the way I am with Jackson. It sounds cheesy but I do feel complete when I'm around him, like a part of me had been missing all these years.

"You look beautiful like this, smiling, carefree. Ask me to move in with you, Elle. One of the best moments of my life was waking up with you and the kids this morning and knowing that I didn't have to sneak out."

"Okay," I say through my smile. "Move in with me, Jackson."

"You mean it?" he gasps.

"I do. I want you here all the time and the kids like having you around."

He kisses me passionately, his excitement pouring through his lips as he melds our mouths together.

"Ew," I hear from beside me and then suddenly a spray of water comes shooting in our direction.

"Well, they just better get used to it because I plan on kissing you every chance I get," Jackson says as he kisses me again and then bounces away, grabbing his water gun and shooting toward the kids.

I sit up in my puddle of mud and grass and watch Jackson and the kids chasing after each other in the yard, running between his yard and mine. Yet all I can think about is that we'll have to put a new fence up after all.

Epilogue

Elle

Five Months Later

Mark and Victoria sway to their first dance as I look up from putting the final touch on their wedding cake. The six-tier monstrosity looks like something out of a fairytale, and after meeting Victoria myself, I knew that she deserved a fairytale and all that came with it.

"Leave it alone, Elle," I hear a deep voice say from behind me.

"But this flower just isn't right."

"Stop. She won't even notice."

"Fine," I huff as I put down the wooden dowel I use to shape flower petals and turn to face Jackson who looks gorgeous in his tuxedo.

"How many potential clients have you spoken to tonight?" he asks as he slides his hands around my waist and rests them just above my ass.

"Two. And one has a cousin tying the knot in a few months."

"Still happy with your decision?"

"Best decision ever."

"I thought me moving in was your best decision ever?" he jokingly questions. I have to keep reminding him that he pretty much asked me to ask him to move in.

Jackson moved his things in right away, as in he was completely moved into my house by that night. We were lucky that his brother was in the market for a house because he is renting Jackson's home. Jackson calls it an investment property.

The kids love having Jackson with us, especially Noah who missed having a man in the house. I heard him one night as he was getting ready for bed telling Jackson that he was scared to take care of his sister and me, he didn't want to mess it up. That broke my heart and I cried into a bottle of wine for hours. Luckily Jackson reminded me that I'm the one that raised such a selfless kid and one day he was going to make a great dad. Then I launched into another sobfest at not wanting my kids to grow up.

It was a rough night.

Another woman stops us and asks for a business card and then lights up when she learns that I make the éclairs for Mark's business. Apparently, she's an associate. After Sara and I poured through contracts, I decided to turn down both offers with Elver's Catering and Beckley's Baked Goods. I didn't like the thought of Elver's owning my recipes, even though my name would be attached, and the idea of having to package my own items for long distance travel on a frequent basis kind of freaked me out.

Instead, I do what everyone has suggested all along – design cakes and continue my online ordering. Since meeting Jackson my recipes and designs have been flourishing, it's as if he's my creative Mecca.

"You ready to get out of here?" Jackson asks as he grabs my jacket and purse from the table. He seems eager, and that makes me a solid mix of nervous and excited. We have a rare night home without the kids who were visiting with Dan, Sky, and their new baby boy this morning, and my parents are picking them up for a sleepover.

Dan has left us alone since I put the restraining order in place and the court forced him to pay the hospital bill that Jackson had covered for me. They also forced him to place the kids back on his insurance. Luckily, my parents don't mind working as the middlemen between Dan and me because they enjoy their time with the kids.

Sara and I have discussed removing the restraining order when the kids get older; we'll see. I still don't trust him, and the relationship he has with Sky is rocky at best, so I'm hoping that he can get his shit together for the sake of their baby.

"Elle?" Jackson asks, bringing me back to the moment. I let my gaze linger on him once again and damn if I'm not the luckiest girl in the room.

"Yes, I'm ready," I reply as I slide into my long dress coat which covers the fuchsia colored gown I'm wearing. I had let Jackson pick it out and he did not disappoint.

He ushers me to the car, and as we pull out of the parking lot, he takes a turn which is the opposite direction of our house.

"Where are we going?"

"I just need to make a pit stop," he says, and continues driving with a smirk on his face.

The signs for the hospital come into view and my heart starts pounding.

"What are we doing here? Are the kids okay?" I ask in panic as I try to pull at the door handles before the car comes to a complete stop.

Calmly he reaches out and grasps my arm. "Everything is okay. I just need to do something inside real quick. Do you want to come with me?"

"Yeah, okay," I whisper as a hundred thoughts swirl through my head, most of which have me wondering what Jackson needs to do at the hospital. Is he sick? Hurt?

He walks up to the receptionist desk and gives the nurse his name and then takes my hand and guides me to some seats in the back corner. We sit quietly for a few minutes, both of our heads turned toward the television across the way. His hand grips mine as he strokes his thumb across the back. It's calming.

"Elle, do you know where we are?"

"Um. . . the hospital?" I reply. Jackson gently shakes his head before sliding from the chair to the ground kneeling before me.

"This exact place is where I fell in love with you. It's where I fell in love with your family. I never saw myself desiring that until I met you.

"You've shown me what it means to be loved and how to show that love so effortlessly. You amaze me, and I would be deeply honored if you would be my wife. Will you marry me, Elle?"

I can barely see him through my tears but I'm nodding my head repeatedly like a bobblehead doll.

"Yes," I finally whisper as he slides a large diamond ring onto my finger, a finger I swore would never wear a decoration again. But that was before I knew Jackson. That was before he snuck into my bedroom that night. That was before I knew what real love is.

I fall into his waiting arms as the crowd around us erupts in applause.

"I can't wait to tell the kids," I say to him, and he chuckles as he seals our lips together before lifting me into his arms.

On the ride home he tells me that he knew months ago that he wanted me to be his wife and he even bought the ring when we were in New York.

"You know something," I begin as he parks the car in front of our house. "I thought that I was one of the unluckiest people in the world when I moved in here. I had lost everything in a divorce, I was willed this terrible house by a father I barely knew, and I had this crazy asshole of a neighbor. But it seems that without any of those things I wouldn't be where I am today – with you."

"Have I ever told you that I want to send Dan a thank you card for being an idiot?"

"No, but that doesn't surprise me."

As we step out of the car, I can hear some moaning coming from Cooper's house and Jackson and I roll our eyes at each other silently wishing that his brother would keep his windows closed at night.

"Who do you think is over there?" I ask, because we never see anyone coming or going from his house.

Suddenly I'm flipped over Jackson's shoulders as he struts up the walkway.

"Don't know, don't care. All I want to do right now is make love to my fiancée."

"Well, why didn't you just say so!"

The End

Acknowledgements

When I wrote my first novel I never expected to be doing this three years later with twelve books under my belt. I went into this book world completely blind and someway, somehow, have figured out how to guide my way through all the craziness that comes with being an author.

Thank you to all of the bloggers that have shared my books and supported me along the way. I appreciate everything that you so behind the scenes and my gratitude for your work is overwhelming.

I want to send a special thanks out to my best friend and PA Renee McCleary. Without you I have no idea where I would be or what I would be doing. You keep me in line and help embrace my craziness. I treasure our friendship more than you'll ever know.

There are a whole list of people that I want to send a special thanks to for coming into my life and supporting me along the way. Amanda Andrews, Teri Kay, Cindy/Thia Finn, Kristine Dugger, Nichole Dennis, Heather Lyn, Crystal Jimenez, Sally Sutherland, Colleen McGrath, Lisa Hemming, Shelly Reynolds, Misty Hamilton, Hayley Michele, Phoenix Soy, Wander Aguiar, my list could go on and on. And if I forgot to mention your name just know that I adore each and every person that I have come in contact with through this journey.

This book wouldn't be half as amazing as I believe it is without the talent of Virginia Tesi Carey. She transformed my words in something so beautiful and eloquent making it far better than I ever could. Thank you for your time and patience with me.

For my husband and family. I won't lie, there are days that I'm sure you all forget what I look like as I hole myself away working on a story. But you continue to encourage me and are just as proud of my fictional world as I am. I absolutely wouldn't have been able to travel down this path without each of you pushing me along the way.

For my children. You are the absolute best, even when you're not. I wouldn't change either one of you even when you delete my words because your "working like Mommy." I love you both to the ends of the Earth.

About the Author

Renee Harless is a romance writer with an affinity for wine and a passion for telling a good story.

Renee Harless, her husband, and children live in Blue Ridge Mountains of Virginia. She studied Communication, specifically Public Relations, at Radford University.

Growing up, Renee always found a way to pursue her creativity. It began by watching endless runs of White Christmas- yes even in the summer – and learning every word and dance from the movie. She could still sing "Sister Sister" if requested. In high school, she joined the show choir and a community theatre group, The Troubadours. After marrying the man of her dreams and moving from her hometown she sought out a different artistic outlet – writing.

To say that Renee is a romance addict would be an understatement. When she isn't chasing her toddler or preschooler around the house, working her day job, or writing, she jumps head first into a romance novel.

www.ingramcontent.com/pod-product-compliance
Lightning Source LLC
Chambersburg PA
CBHW022024120726
47898CB00007BA/2102